HANDSOME HOTSHOT

LORI WILDE
LIZ ALVIN

❧ 1 ❧

"Michael, I've got an opportunity for you."

Michael Parker looked up from his computer as his boss, Nathan Barrett, walked into his office. At the word "opportunity," he froze, wary about what would happen next.

"Opportunity?" He didn't like the sound of this. In business, the word opportunity was just another way of saying huge, horrible mess. It was sort of like telling folks on a sinking ship they would have the opportunity to practice swimming in the ocean.

"Calm down." Nathan chuckled and sat in the chair facing Michael's desk. "It's not a terrible thing."

Even if it was, Michael knew he would find a way around this problem. He always did. Wrangling problems was his specialty.

"How can I help?" he asked.

"That's it exactly. Remember during your interview when we discussed community involvement? That's why I'm here. So you can help."

"I'm lost."

Nathan smiled. "I want all senior managers to volunteer at least ten hours a week for the next couple of months. By the managers volunteering, I'm hoping the staff will as well."

"Volunteer?" Michael frowned, confused, which happened often these days. This company, especially his boss Nathan Barrett, was unlike any other place he'd worked before. The atmosphere in the office was very casual, even relaxed. Anything could happen, which meant this opportunity might really end up biting him.

"Volunteer?" he repeated.

"Yep. Now before you start worrying, you can go during your regular office hours. I'm not looking to cut into your life."

"I see," he said, but truthfully, he didn't at all. For starters, he had no life outside of work, and he was happiest that way.

"See, here's the thing," Nathan said. "I love the town of Honey, Texas. It's where I grew up and where I built my company. Our company is thriving, and I want Honey to thrive as well. You like Honey, don't you?"

Michael had to think about his answer. He'd been born and raised in a small Texas town, even smaller than Honey, and he'd forgotten how much he disliked it—until he'd moved here. Everyone meddled in everyone's business. "Um, it's interesting."

His comment made Nathan laugh. "Let me guess, you're not used to having people stop and analyze the contents of your cart at the grocery store."

Analyze. Comment. Criticize. Yes, he didn't appreciate any of it. "They do take an interest," was all he said.

"Yep. It's great, right?" Nathan asked.

"Sure." Michael knew better than to criticize something, anything, that was important to his boss. He'd worked his way through college and through five years at an accounting firm by knowing how to make his boss' priorities his priorities.

"You grew up in a small town, right? So that interest probably wasn't a surprise," Nathan said.

Michael hated talking about where he grew up, but he didn't show it. "Yes, it is a very small town. Just one stoplight."

"Honey now has three! Bet it looks like a big city to you." Nathan's smile showed he absolutely did not understand how Michael had felt about his hometown. It was a dusty, dry piece of West Texas dirt.

"So about this mandatory volunteering," Michael said, wanting to avoid talking about his hometown with the same zeal that a cat avoided a bath.

The grin on Nathan's face made it clear that he understood what Michael was doing. But he let it slide. Instead, he said, "You've only been here a little over a month. Give it time. You'll grow to love Honey once you put down roots."

Michael was more likely to believe that armadillos could square dance than to believe he'd come to love Honey, but he simply said, "I'm sure."

Nathan seemed to find this response funny because he laughed. "That's one of the other great things about volunteering. You'll get to learn more about Honey and the people who live here. I want you to volunteer at the Honey Senior Citizen Center. You'll really get to know the local folks by helping out there."

Only years of practice enabled Michael to stop a horrified expression from crossing his face. A senior citizen center? Him? Around old, retired people?

"Couldn't I just give them a donation?" he tried, feeling like a drowning man hoping for a life preserver.

Nathan shook his head. "No. I want you to be hands-on. You are not allowed to give them money. Just your time."

The focus should be on making money, not wasting time volunteering. "Shouldn't we spend our time looking for ways to expand? The company's doing great, but I think now is the best time to look for other opportunities. We've got the merger to focus on."

Nathan nodded. "I know, and we'll do that too. We'll find the time."

Michael struggled to keep himself from pointing out the obvious. Every day had a limited number of hours. He couldn't waste his puttering around with old people.

"Don't worry. It's all going to work out fine," Nathan said, standing and heading toward the door. "Just swing by today for a little while on your way home. I think you'll find you enjoy helping out and meeting more of the residents of Honey."

With that, Nathan walked out.

Michael watched him leave, a feeling of doom settling over him. Oh, he was all for charity and gave often. He knew firsthand what it meant to rely on strangers for help. But giving money was different from giving time. Money he had, time he didn't.

Despite what Nathan said, you couldn't make time. It was limited, and a long time ago, he'd promised himself that he would use all his time to make sure he got ahead in life.

He was in the process of examining several companies for a potential major merger, and if he pulled it off, Barrett Software would be set for years.

And if he failed...

Ah, but he wouldn't. Failure was not an option. So he wouldn't fail. He wouldn't allow himself to fail. And once he pulled off this look-Ma-no-hands major miracle, it would be pretty much guaranteed that he could move to an even bigger corporation and an even bigger paycheck.

He was going to find a way to turn this opportunity into a true opportunity.

Nothing—and no one—was going to stop his climb to the top. He'd build a snowman with the devil before he allowed himself to fail. It just flat out would not happen.

"So, what are you going to do with him?"

Casey Richards hunkered under her ancient metal desk, trying to shove a piece of cardboard beneath the short leg. At the words, she rose to her knees and looked over the desktop.

Elmira Ross, a dedicated regular at the Honey Senior Citizen Center, stood in her doorway. Elmira was what the gentlemen called a looker. Even at seventy, she still turned heads with an irresistible combination of a devilish personality and the most unusual azure eyes.

"Do with whom?" Casey asked, refolding the square of cardboard.

"The new guy. Rumor has it we're getting a new man today. I bet he's a handsome devil."

Rumor would be Tommy Gilbert. Or Albert Terford. Or any of the other gentlemen who were infatuated with Elmira.

"The new guy, as you call him, is a volunteer," Casey said.

Elmira grinned, showing dimples that had probably broken more than a few hearts in her lifetime. "Oh, honey, you don't fool me. I know he's a young one. Why do you think I'm so interested? He could be perfect for you."

Casey didn't want to encourage Elmira, but she couldn't prevent herself from smiling. This was what she loved about being the director of the center—the regulars were a great group of people.

But she needed to be clear on this point, so Casey said, "Don't try to matchmake. This man is here to help the center."

The older woman shrugged. "You're part of the center."

"Not a part that needs fixing," Casey stressed.

"Oh, Casey, men are like hats. No woman really needs one, and on certain days, they're more trouble than they're worth. But if you're lucky enough to find the perfect one, then your life will be truly blessed."

Despite herself, Casey laughed. "I don't want or need a hat. Moreover, Michael Parker is not a hat. He's a hotshot exec from Barrett Software. I don't need a hotshot creating problems. I need a volunteer helping with solutions."

Just thinking about having a corporate exec here made Casey cringe. Sure, the center could use all the volunteers it could get. Heck, she encouraged companies to have their employees volunteer, and no company had helped out as much as Barrett Software.

But having one of their executives here was the last thing she needed.

Especially since she knew he'd been forced to volunteer. The man wouldn't want to be here. Men like him never wanted to be anywhere but at work. He'd probably end up being about as much help as using a thimble to bail out a sinking ship.

"I refuse to believe this man won't liven things up around here," Elmira said. "If he's an executive, then maybe he'll give us some help with financial planning."

As much as Casey would love Mr. Corporate Hatchetman to give the seniors financial advice, he probably would only know how to work with a budget in the billions.

Plus, his own finances would be so convoluted with stock options and bonuses and incentives that he wouldn't have a clue as to what life on social security and meager savings was like.

But she didn't say this to Elmira. Instead, she shrugged. "We can always hope for the best."

With a final smile at the older woman, she ducked back under her desk and shoved the cardboard beneath the leg. It still wasn't enough. Groaning, she scooted around until she found a more comfortable position, then set about refolding the cardboard.

When she heard someone lift the phone receiver and punch in numbers, she hollered, "That better not be a long-distance number you're dialing. This phone isn't like your cell phone. These calls cost."

"It's not a long-distance call," a man's voice said.

Casey frowned. Although male, the voice definitely belonged to a younger man. He wasn't one of the seniors. She squirmed out from underneath her desk, bumping her head at the last second.

"Shoot." Half scooting, half crawling, she managed an undignified exit from under the desk, rocked back on her heels, and looked up.

There was no doubt about the identity of the man standing on the other side of her desk. The expensive navy suit gave him away.

He stood talking on her phone as if this were his office, not hers. She slowly rose to her feet and tried to brush off the dark smear across the front of her T-shirt, then gave up.

The man watched her with open amusement. He had great eyes. An interesting, almost warm, cerulean blue. Those eyes gave him a sincerity that had undoubtedly helped him in corporate takeovers and ruthless downsizings.

He'd look across at his prey, and they wouldn't realize their days were numbered. They'd get suckered in by the twinkle in those baby blues, and before they knew what happened, *kapow,* they'd be history!

Yep, she'd give him this—he was a good-looking corporate shark. Elmira had been right. He was a handsome devil. Easily over six feet, with midnight-black hair that was brushed back from his tanned face. A striking face with a square jaw and a tiny cleft in his chin.

Bet he pays more for a haircut than I pay for a week's groceries, Casey thought, studying him while he rattled off numbers like a calculator.

When he simply nodded at her and continued with his conversation, Casey decided enough was enough. She leaned across her small desk and tapped on the phone.

"We only have one line. You need to end this call. I'm waiting for an important call from a potential donor, and I don't want it to roll to voicemail."

He raised his hand in an obvious signal asking for a few more minutes.

"I need those revised figures on my desk by five tonight, Glenda. I can't wait until morning." He looked at his slim, gold watch. "I'll be through here by four-thirty."

Annoyed, Casey tapped the phone again. "I'm not trying to be rude, but you can't tie up this line," she repeated, her voice louder this time.

Okay, cute was one thing, but this big-business jock was about to turn into her worst nightmare. He'd only been here twelve seconds, and he'd already yanked her chain by trying to take over.

Sheesh.

Sure, she'd admit that a man like Michael Parker could swing a lot of clout with other companies. And sure, he probably could help her rustle up donations. But there was also a really good chance he wouldn't help her at all. He might just spend all his time on her phone doing his work if she didn't stop him. And she would stop him.

She needed to take a stand and take it now.

Without asking again, she calmly reached across the desk and depressed the button on her battered black phone. Then she waited for the fireworks.

"What the hell do you—"

She held up one hand, halting his words. "First off, we do not curse in this building. That will cost you a dollar. In the future, I expect you to find a more appropriate way to express yourself."

"Who in the hell—"

"I mean it. You now owe me two dollars." She met his steely gaze with one of her own. Granted, her own five-foot-seven height put her at a disadvantage. But she'd been raised by a corporate shark, so she knew how to stare down the best of them.

"Two dollars?"

"I assume you're Michael Parker." She quirked one eyebrow and waited for his answer.

"Yes." From his expression, he was grappling with a lot of emotions, not the least of which she guessed was anger. This man needed to be hung up on. In her opinion, it was long overdue.

He motioned toward her phone. "Look, I realize you've just got the one line, but that's a vital phone call. I'll only be a few minutes."

A reasonable person would say yes, sure, he could use the phone. But Casey really needed to be able to answer the call from Honey Dry Cleaners to see if they were going to donate.

Plus, she knew if she said yes now, he'd live on the phone, and she'd never get a bit of work done. And she needed to work. Someone had to do something about raising money for the new Senior Citizen Center. The Victorian house on Lake Hoffler was perfect for a new center.

But so far, the city was only willing to allocate three hundred thousand dollars, which would pay for the house, but not the renovations. She had to come up with the rest of the money before the lease ran out on this building in two months.

If she couldn't come up with the money for renovations, then the whole project would go down the drain.

So even though refusing Michael Parker today might seem petty, she needed every spare second she could find to hunt up donors.

"Why don't you just use your cell phone to make your call?" she asked.

He sighed. "Something's wrong with it. It's charged and it still rings, but I can't make calls or receive them." His hand snaked toward her phone. "So, if you'll just give me a couple of minutes."

The man was like a junkie needing a phone fix. She watched his fingers wrap around the receiver. "I'm afraid I can't do that. I need the phone. It's very important I round up donations."

He didn't relax his grip. "Well, my call won't hold you up for long." He lifted the phone a couple of inches. "I'll be off in plenty of time for you to make your own calls."

Casey's temper flared, but she tapped it down. No way would she lose this fight. If she did, it would set a terrible precedent. "You're here to help, not to use the phone."

He smiled, a smooth, no doubt well-used smile. Oh, it was a good one. Just enough sincerity and little-boy mischief in it to make Casey's pulse kick up a notch. Tiny lines fanned out from his eyes, making him even more attractive.

"I'm not trying to be difficult," he said.

Yeah. Right. And she had some swampland that would look great on a vacation postcard. "But you're succeeding, all the same."

That got him. His smile dimmed just a fraction. She could almost see him reevaluating her. He hadn't expected her to stand up to him.

"How about if I promise that the next time I come, I'll bring my own phone?"

Casey drummed her fingernails on the desk, the staccato pings unusually loud in her tiny office. Frankly, she was torn between wanting to be reasonable and wanting to stand her ground. She had enough goddess-warrior in her to want to win this battle, to be triumphant, to rule the day. A glance around her office brought her back to reality.

"Tell you what...you can use my phone today for

exactly ten minutes if you make a donation to help renovate our new building."

Like a light being switched off, Michael's smile faded. "You're charging me to use the phone?"

"Not charging, exactly. Let's just say that during those ten minutes, I might have been lucky enough to find someone who would be happy to make a sizable donation to the center."

At the word sizable, a frown formed on Michael's face. "You can't be serious. Chances are, in those ten minutes, you wouldn't even have gotten anyone to agree."

He had a point, but she wasn't about to admit it. Truthfully, she rarely had luck getting help from local companies.

She smiled benignly. No sense telling Mr. Hotshot that.

"Actually, I've made quite a few good contacts in the community over the past couple of months," she said. "I'm sure I can get lots of donations. Now, about using the phone—"

"Ah, hell."

Casey shook her finger. "Mr. Parker, I've warned you about the language. The tally's up to three dollars."

For a split second, the manager mask on his face lifted, and she could see how thoroughly exasperated he was with her. Then the mask dropped back into place.

"Fine. You win. This phone call is dam—um, important, so I'll make a donation. How much?"

How much? Shoot, she hadn't thought that far ahead. She was winging this and hadn't really expected him to agree. She'd thought he'd just storm out.

So, how much? She studied his watch. Thin. Gold. Expensive. "One hundred dollars."

He visibly blanched. "What? Are you crazy? I'm not giving you a damn cent."

That was it. Casey walked around her desk until she stood directly in front of Michael Parker. Then she straightened her spine to take advantage of what height she did have. Finally, she made eye contact with him.

"That makes it four dollars. And if you curse in this building one more time, I'm going to reject you as a volunteer. It's my understanding that your boss, Nathan Barrett, specifically wanted you to work at the Honey Senior Citizen Center. I imagine he'll be unhappy if you get fired your first day on the job."

As she expected, he didn't quail at her words. "I'm not afraid of Nathan, so there's no point threatening me. I'm also a volunteer here, so you need me more than I need you."

"Not true. I don't need someone who's more interested in using my phone than in helping the seniors. We've been just hunky-dory without you until now, and we'll do just peachy-keen without you in the future. So, Mr. Parker, what will it be? My phone for a hundred, or shall I call Nathan and tell him things didn't work out?"

As he stood watching her, she noticed a slight shifting in his features. Some muscles tightened; others loosened. On another man, she'd say his expression was one of admiration. But as far as she could tell, Michael Parker didn't admire her. He viewed her as a small obstacle in his way.

But she knew, long before he reached into the inside pocket of his jacket and withdrew his leather checkbook, she'd won this battle. Inside, her stomach did a quick flip-flop. She'd actually won.

"One hundred in exchange for using the phone whenever I want during the next two hours," he said, bending down to write the check.

Casey thought for a moment. A reasonable woman would take the check and run. But the little devil inside her wouldn't leave things alone. She opened her mouth before she could consider the wisdom of pushing a brick wall.

"One hundred and you can use the phone for no more than thirty minutes while you're here today."

He paused, his hand frozen holding the pen above the pale-green check. He didn't look at her. Didn't say a thing. Then, slowly, he lowered his hand and wordlessly wrote the check.

Casey felt like she'd won the lottery. When he finished writing, he tore the check out of the book and handed it to her.

"You can make it out to whomever you want. The

center. A handyman." He tipped his head and gave her a pointed look. "Or maybe you'd just as soon make it out to yourself."

Casey smiled. "Why, Mr. Parker, we barely know each other, and you've already formed such a sweet opinion of me. I'm thoroughly delighted with all of your character traits, too."

His lips lifted at the corners just a tad. "How does anyone survive around you without cursing?"

"They use their imaginations." She glanced at the check and then held out her hand. "You still owe me four dollars."

As he reached for his wallet, he muttered, "Bass fishing."

Casey chuckled and snatched the four dollars from his hand. "See. I knew you'd find a way to stop cursing." She tucked the check and the dollars in an envelope. "Now, thanks to you, I've made a great start on the renovations fund."

Michael Parker leaned against her desk, but when it wobbled, he straightened. "I'm only praying you're Casey Richards, the director here."

She extended her hand. "Yes. I can't tell you what a pleasure it's been to meet you, Mr. Parker."

He took her hand and shook it firmly. The handshake was swift and professional, but still, a tingle ran up her arm at the contact. Normally, that reaction told her she was attracted to a man. But in Michael Parker's case, she'd assume the tingle was static electricity. She'd never been attracted to a corporate shark in her life, and she wasn't about to start now.

Casey released Michael's hand and stepped back a half step. "I hope you enjoy working here, Mr. Parker."

He picked up the phone. "Call me Michael. I like to be on a first-name basis with people who take me for that much money."

🏵 2 🏵

Michael watched Casey walk out of the office and felt like kicking himself. He'd broken his number one rule—never underestimate an opponent. In fact, at first he hadn't even realized Casey Richards was an opponent. And who could blame him?

When she'd crawled out from under the desk, she'd looked like a pushover. An incredibly sexy pushover, with wavy auburn hair that hung to the middle of her back and large green eyes in a pretty oval face.

Rounding out the tempting package was a gently curved shape in worn jeans. That shape made his mind wander off in dangerous directions.

Yeah, he'd underestimated Casey, all right. He'd figured the director would be some nice quiet woman he could convince to let him do his work while he was here.

Not all the time, of course. He'd live up to his side of the deal and help out. But come on, he couldn't spend ten hours a week ignoring the office. He was tracking too many projects to waste a good part of each week playing bingo.

He glanced at his watch, then punched in the phone number of his assistant, Glenda Myers. Thank God she was back at the office keeping things running. He'd give this harebrained scheme one week at the most. Then Nathan would see the huge hit to productivity the company was taking, and he'd have to rescind this order.

Michael knew all he had to do was survive a week or two. He'd been through worse—like the layoffs at his past employer. This charity work would be a piece of cake.

While he waited for Glenda to answer, he glanced out the open office door and watched Casey working in the main room. She hadn't been what he'd expected, granted, but he had to admit he admired her. Not many people stood up to him anymore.

He knew how to stare them down, but his best techniques hadn't worked with her. Which surprised him. The woman spent her days working with retirees. He wouldn't expect her to know the first thing about negotiating.

But she had. She'd negotiated him out of a hundred bucks. Although, to be honest, he'd probably have given her the money anyway, just to smooth things out over the next few days. In his experience, charity types loved you to pieces once you gave them a nice fat donation.

He continued with his phone call for quite some time before an odd sensation made him look out into the main room again. Casey caught his gaze. He expected her to smile, but she didn't. Instead, she frowned at him, tapped the chunky watch on her wrist, and then held up five fingers.

He glanced at his own watch, a present last year from his previous employer for a killer deal he'd worked. With a sigh, he realized the woman was right —he only had five minutes left.

A hundred dollars sure didn't buy what it used to.

❦

"I told you he was a handsome devil."

Casey spun around to find Elmira and her best friend, Dottie, directly behind her. The women stood watching Michael Parker through her open office door. Casey followed their gazes.

These two ladies might be seniors, but there was nothing wrong with their eyesight or their judgment. Michael Parker certainly qualified as a handsome devil, but he personified everything Casey disliked in a man.

"He's okay," she admitted, knowing Elmira and Dottie wouldn't swallow a lie. "But if he thinks he's going to spend all of his time on the phone, he's wrong."

The two women trailed after her as she moved the chairs to make room for the birthday celebration due to start in a few minutes. "My Bernie was that good-looking," Dottie said.

Elmira rolled her eyes. "Dottie, Bernie was barely over five feet tall. He didn't look a thing like that man does."

Rather than being offended, Dottie laughed. "Okay, so Bernie wasn't tall. But he was still great-looking. And he knew a thing or two about romance."

Elmira nudged Casey. "Do you think that handsome devil over there knows a thing or two about romance?"

Despite herself, Casey looked at Michael and pondered the question. He had the looks to make a woman's heart race. And the self-confidence. The question was whether he ever slowed down long enough to make the experience memorable. Would he linger over each caress? Hover over each kiss?

Her gaze dropped to his mouth, which currently was in a tight, straight line. He wasn't happy about something. Casey watched his lips as he spoke. What would it feel like to have a man like that whisper seductive words in her ear?

"I think we've sent her into a tailspin," Elmira observed.

Casey blinked and looked at the two women, embarrassed by her daydreams. "I need to get back to work."

Dottie smiled. "Sure you do, dear. Don't let us get in your way."

Casey hurriedly pushed some of the tables together and replaced the chairs. She ignored the quiet conversation Dottie and Elmira held in the corner of the room and instead headed to the kitchen to put candles on the birthday cake.

She didn't really need to hear them to know they were still discussing Michael Parker. Dottie and Elmira had a long history of interfering in her love life. Both ladies thought it was beyond time Casey settled down.

So far, they'd offered up all their grandsons and one great-nephew, but to no avail. Casey had a specific type of man in mind, a home-loving man who adored children. The successful grandsons traveled all the time.

And the great-nephew disliked children.

But those failures hadn't slowed down Elmira and Dottie. If anything, the more men Casey rejected, the more the two women seemed determined to find a match.

They felt by the advanced age of twenty-eight, if Casey didn't marry soon, she'd die alone. And as Elmira liked to point out, the older Casey got, the smaller the fishing pond became.

Casey glanced back at her office. Speaking of fish, or actually sharks, there was a corporate shark who needed to be told a thing or two. No sense putting it off any longer. She had to get back in her office and settle the ground rules.

Mr. Michael Parker needed to know straight out who was the boss here. He might be a bigwig at his office, but at the Honey Senior Citizen Center, he was just one more volunteer to help during the birthday party.

***

Of all the times not to be able to cuss. Michael ran an agitated hand through his hair while Glenda related the latest disaster. He felt like a pressure cooker about to explode. If he didn't vent some of his frustration soon, things were not going to be pretty.

Out of the corner of his eye, he noticed Casey Richards appear in the doorway. He wasn't halfway through his conversation with Glenda, but he knew better than to push his luck. He'd just have to stay at the office really late tonight to catch up on work.

"Look, Glenda, I've got to go. The warden is here." He glanced over his shoulder at Casey. She wasn't smiling, but she wasn't frowning, either. She met his amused gaze straight on, and then walked into her office and sat behind her desk.

With a couple of final words, he hung up the phone and took the chair across from Casey. The tiny desk put hardly any space between them, and it gave her no psychological advantage at all.

"You need a bigger desk," he observed, putting his day planner back in his briefcase. "Hel—" He froze, ignored her raised eyebrows, and continued, "Heck, you need a bigger office. This whole building, in fact, is way too small for the activities you have planned here."

She leaned forward. "Mr. Parker—"

"I already told you, it's Michael."

"Okay, Michael. I explained I'm in the process of getting a new building for the center. But the size of my office and desk is the least of my concerns. What does concern me is what you intend on doing while you're volunteering here."

Straight to the point. He liked directness in a business associate, and he appreciated it in Casey. He briefly studied her, noting again how attractive she was. Of course, Casey's appearance shouldn't concern him.

She wasn't his type. He liked women who were equally intent on their careers. Women who knew how to handle themselves at a business dinner. Certainly not red-haired social-worker types with big green eyes.

"What did you think volunteering at the center would mean?"

He shrugged. "Helping do whatever it is you do, I guess." He shifted forward in his chair. "I suppose you know the purpose of my being here is to encourage other Barrett Software employees to get involved with the community."

"Will these employees be able to volunteer during office hours like you are?"

He was pretty sure there was censure behind her words, although nothing in her tone backed up his suspicions. "Of course. Nathan made it clear they would be given time to help out. In my case, it doesn't really matter. If I'm not asleep, I'm working. Basically, all of the hours in my day are office hours."

She watched him intently. Something about the way she studied him told him she didn't like him much. Which was stupid, considering he'd just given the woman a hundred dollars for her new building. But he couldn't shake the feeling she viewed him as a distasteful pile she'd stepped in.

"Look, I certainly can use volunteers, but only if they're sincerely interested in helping. If you're just here to make your boss happy, then—"

"I plan on helping," he interjected. At her dubious expression, he added, "Okay, I'll admit I'd rather not spend a good part of each week here. Still, I'll do my best to help."

"Good," was all she said in a tight little voice that let him know loud and clear that she was still ticked off. Casey should never play poker—he could read her every emotion on her expressive face.

Leaning back in his chair, he considered her. People like Casey Richards baffled him. Why work so hard for something that personally got you nowhere? It didn't make sense.

"So, what can I do to help out while I'm here?" he asked.

"I don't know. What skills do you have?"

The way she asked, in short, clipped syllables, made him think she felt he had no skills. Or at least none that would be of use to her.

"I'm great at managing things."

She arched one eyebrow. "Things?"

"People."

She nodded. "So I gathered." She placed her arms on the wobbly desk in front of her. He looked at her hands. No rings. Short nails. A practical woman.

"This afternoon, please help with the birthday party. We have one for each senior every year. You'll find the decorations on the top shelf of the cabinet in the kitchen."

The idea of helping seniors with a party didn't appeal to him. Truth was, he didn't know what to say to the people here. He'd never known his grandparents, his mother had left when he'd been two, and his father had died years ago.

Outside of work, Michael didn't know anyone over the age of fifty. What did you talk about to people who no longer worked?

This idea didn't appeal to him at all. "And after the party?"

"Then you can call some of your executive friends and manage them in the direction of their checkbooks. We need some serious donations."

With that, she left her office.

Michael watched her go. Great. Just great. Not only did he get to waste a large part of his week helping out around here, but now he got to hassle all of his associates.

No doubt about it—he had to get out of this place soon.

❧ 3 ❧

Michael drew in a deep breath, bit back yet another curse, and blew up the twenty-third big, bright balloon in a pack of twenty-five. Two more after this. Only two more balloons to go, and he'd be done.

He shot a quick glance across the room at Casey, who was talking to some of the seniors. Of course, she'd put him in charge of the party decorations. Especially balloons. She obviously thought he had hot air to spare.

"Your face is almost as red as that balloon."

Michael glanced at the older man who had come to stand next to him. "Yeah, I'm afraid I'm going to collapse a lung," Michael said.

The man chuckled. "I'm the birthday boy, Al Terford." Idly, he pushed some of the balloons across the table. A few tumbled with drunken abandon onto the floor. "Balloons. Now there's an odd touch. What are you going to do with these when you're done?"

Michael froze, some little internal gizmo dinging crazily inside his head. He turned and nailed Al with a direct gaze. "Don't you usually have balloons at these parties?"

Al chuckled again. "Well, no. We're kind of old for balloons. But I appreciate the gesture."

Michael looked at the balloon in his hands, replaying his conversation with Casey through his mind. She'd told him to put out the things for the party, indicated the cabinet where the supplies were stored, and explained he'd find everything he needed inside. And he had. On the top shelf, he'd found cups, plates, and napkins.

Then two shelves down...balloons.

Ah, hell. Glancing up, he caught Casey looking his direction. She'd watched him blow up all these balloons and make an idiot of himself in front of the seniors. He should be mad. Furious, in fact.

But he wasn't. Instead, he found himself half admiring her. Okay, the lady was quickly becoming a personal pain in the butt to him. Still, he'd been at the center for what? Less than an hour. And the woman had already bested him. Twice.

The next couple of weeks should prove very interesting.

"You have to watch the women around here," Al pointed out. "They're sharp, so you have to be sharper."

With those words, the older man patted Michael's shoulder then wandered over to the table where Casey was lighting candles on a cake. When he finished knotting the last balloon, he settled back to watch the celebration.

All the seniors were having a great time. Casey was having a great time, too. Michael watched, fascinated, as she kidded around with the group. She really fit in here, but he couldn't help wondering why she wasn't working at a big company, making big bucks.

"Having fun?" Casey asked when she finally wandered over in his direction.

"I enjoyed blowing up all those balloons. Thanks."

Casey laughed. It was a teasing, light sound that ran across his skin like a touch. "Sorry. But I didn't tell you to do it. We used those balloons at our booth at the children's fair last September. I never thought you'd dig them out, but they do add a festive air. Now, why don't you stop sulking and come mingle? No one's going to bite you."

"I'm not afraid," Michael said slowly, but the truth was, he'd never been too comfortable around older people. Nathan knew that, which was no doubt why he'd been assigned to the Honey Senior Citizen Center.

But rather than explain that to Casey, Michael changed the subject. "So you have birthday parties for everyone, do you?"

"Yes. It's vital to mark the major moments in the lives of those you care about."

Michael sensed there was more to what she was saying, but before he could press her on it, a loud squawking noise silenced the room. Every head turned toward him. Michael groaned and fished his phone out of his pocket.

Glancing at it, he saw that Glenda was calling. When he looked up at Casey, her frown told him how she felt about the interruption.

"I thought your phone didn't work," she said.

He sighed. "It still rings, but I can't answer the calls or make calls. So, may I please use your phone one more time?"

Casey smiled at the group of seniors watching them. "Nothing serious. Michael's got a hectic job," she told them. When the seniors resumed talking, she stepped forward until she stood directly in front of him. Then she said in a whisper, "Make your call. But next time you come here, please don't spend all your time on the phone, neither on the center's phone or your cell phone."

"Look, I'm not trying to—"

"You should respect the seniors enough to give them your complete attention while you're here. But you corporate jocks just don't get it, do you? You can't let go of your job for even a couple of hours."

Ouch. Where'd that come from? "I take it you don't like businessmen," he said.

She fixed him with a narrowed gaze. "I believe there's more to life than work."

He'd heard that song before, from a father who couldn't bring himself to show up for a job on a regular basis. But he knew Casey wasn't talking about goofing off to avoid work. No, she was smack-dab in the middle of her own personal anti-business agenda, and he needed to tread carefully here.

He scanned the amused faces assembled around the collection of tables. Everyone in the room was watching him. Now he knew how a butterfly stuck on a pin felt.

When he returned his gaze to Casey, he said, "Sorry." And he was. He didn't mean to give her flak, and he didn't mean to be disrespectful to the seniors. But this was a strange new world he'd entered, and adjusting would take some time.

Casey was silent for several long moments. Finally, she waved toward her office. "Go make your call. And after that, you might as well stay in there and make those calls for donations, too."

Deciding to leave well enough alone, Michael nodded and headed toward the office. This was hard. He wasn't used to feeling uncertain, but he sure did around Casey and the seniors. His gut instinct told him the next couple of weeks were going to be bumpy.

An hour later, Casey was still annoyed. She glanced toward her office repeatedly and watched Michael as he talked on the phone.

Wanting to postpone her talk with him, she headed toward the kitchen to count the hot lunches that had just been delivered. When the number was wrong the first time, she hoped she'd made a mistake.

But when she got the same total once more, she was ready to chew out the delivery service. This couldn't have happened again. They were two lunches short.

She ran her hand through her hair. "Shoot."

The county supplied hot lunches to the center each day as long as she told them twenty-four hours ahead of time how many lunches she needed. The last couple of weeks, the number had been off more often than not.

Sheesh. How hard was it to count to twenty-seven? Heck, yesterday she'd deliberately phoned and faxed in the order to avoid any errors.

Yet, still it was wrong. Didn't the county understand that for many of the seniors, this hot lunch was the main meal of the day? How could they just flub the number?

Her head felt as if little imps were playing bongos on her brain. Idly, she rubbed her temples and looked for a place to sit. Her choices were limited.

The kitchen was ground zero, the worst area in the center. The counters were bowed; the linoleum was frayed, and two of the cabinets no longer opened.

Boy, did the center need a new home. A bright modern home with up-to-date facilities.

And a breathtaking view. Okay, so that wasn't absolutely necessary, but once she'd seen the old Victorian on the lake, she couldn't think of moving the center any place else.

The seniors could sit and watch the sailboats, enjoy the cool breezes of spring, and wander the manicured trails around the lake. Even the city council had agreed it made the perfect location, far better than anything else anyone had found.

Except even with the family who owned it cutting the cost, the price was too high. The council would pay the three hundred thousand for the house if she came up with fifty thousand for modifications. Her share might as well have been a million.

Casey moved over to the door and looked across the main room to her office. She couldn't see Michael Parker, but she knew he was there. Working—probably doing his own work rather than making calls for the center. Objectively, he was exactly what she needed. He was a high-profile executive who could pull in large contributions and plenty of volunteers. Someone used to running big projects could come in very handy.

But she hated the fact that she needed him. Images of her work-obsessed parents filtered through her mind. The missed birthday parties. The forgotten school plays. The never-ending stream of excuses.

Until one day her folks just stopped explaining. Or caring.

She glanced again at her office. Did Michael Parker care about anything? Would he help them even if he could?

Or was he like her parents, just another workaholic who had lost interest a long time ago?

❧

"Why are you hiding in here?"

Michael glanced up. Two elderly women stood in the office doorway, giving him what could only be described as the once-over. He straightened in his chair.

"I'm not hiding. I'm raising money for the building." Some long-forgotten tidbit of protocol nudged at his brain, and he rose.

He never stood when a woman entered a room. If he did, he'd spend most of his days on his feet. Well over half of the employees he dealt with were women. But, admittedly, not women like the two standing just within the doorway. These women weren't associates and were making him feel as uncomfortable as an antelope walking by a bunch of lions.

"See, I told you he wasn't hiding." The woman on the left took a couple of steps forward. "I'm Elmira Ross, and this is Dottie Stevenson."

Neither woman made a move to shake his hand, so Michael stuffed his fists in his pockets.

"It's nice to meet you." He shot a glance back at the phone. Since Casey had left him here, he'd managed to scrounge up another four hundred in donations. Unfortunately, the donations had come from two coworkers at his previous job, who would probably reciprocate by making him buy from their children's school fundraisers for the next twenty years.

He didn't say anything else, mostly because he had no idea what to say. He didn't want to offend the women because they seemed nice.

Still, he couldn't help hoping they would take the hint and leave him alone. Truthfully, they made him jumpy. Funny how he could speak to a convention center filled with employees but was struck mute by two elderly women.

How ironic.

But rather than leave, Dottie moved over next to Elmira.

"Why don't you come out and meet some of the folks? Everyone is interested in you," Dottie said.

Michael's gaze darted beyond the women to the main room outside the office. After the party had ended, the tables had been shifted back into place. Now about twenty older people sat in small groups. Some were playing cards. Others were knitting. Everyone seemed busy, and no one seemed the least bit interested in him.

Except for the two ladies standing in front of him now.

"I...promised Casey I'd make some phone calls." He reached for the phone, praying the women would finally leave. But they didn't. They stood firmly rooted and continued to study him with open curiosity.

"So, what does your wife think about you working here?"

This question came from Dottie, who immediately received a nudge and a stern look from Elmira.

"You don't have to answer that," Elmira said. "Dottie's nosy."

"Oh, and you're not interested?" Dottie asked her friend. Before Elmira could answer, Dottie turned and smiled at him. "A handsome man like you has to be married."

An unexpected smile tugged at the corner of his mouth. Dottie was buttering him up like a Thanksgiving turkey.

"I'm not married." He lifted the receiver, but still, neither woman moved.

"Really? Not married." Elmira exchanged a look with Dottie that Michael didn't even want to begin to interpret. "Casey isn't married, either."

Her comment surprised him so much he had to struggle to keep his jaw from dropping. These women were here to matchmake?

They didn't know a thing about him except he wasn't married, and yet they thought that information was sufficient to toss him in Casey's direction. He scanned the main room, looking for the subject of this discussion. He'd bet his stock options Casey didn't know these two ladies were in here trying to fix her up.

Suddenly curious about the red-haired director, he replaced the receiver, then leaned against the desk and smiled at the women.

This information river flowed two ways. Maybe he could find out what made Casey Richards tick. In his experience, negotiations were easier if you understood your adversary. If he knew what mattered most to Casey, then he'd know what kind of bargain he could strike.

"Casey seems nice," he said, watching the women closely to see what reaction he got. As expected, their faces brightened, and they moved forward, eager to share information.

"Casey's a doll," Dottie offered. "Simply a doll." Her smile faded a tiny bit. "But don't get on her bad side. She's no fool, and she doesn't take kindly to people who play games with her."

"That's right. Never mess around with our Casey," Elmira added. "She deserves only the best." Elmira shifted even closer, a fairly predatory look on her face. "Now, tell us all about you."

Michael tensed. Good Lord. What had he gotten himself into?

Michael finally finagled his way out of the office and

the inquisition Dottie and Elmira were conducting by claiming he'd promised to help Casey.

In a way, his excuse was true, especially since the women had warned him about getting on Casey's bad side. Life had taught him not to make an enemy out of a potential ally. He felt compelled to smooth things over with Casey before he created more hard feelings.

He found her in the kitchen, stacking covered plates and muttering to herself. Unable to resist, he leaned against the doorjamb and watched her work.

Casey Richards might be the thorn in his paw for the next few weeks, but she was also one heck of a sight, especially her long hair. It cascaded like a waterfall down her back, swaying with her movements.

From nowhere, a crazy desire hit him. He wanted to walk over to her, slide his arms around her trim waist, and bury his face in her glorious hair. He could easily see it in his mind. She'd lean back against him, sighing. Then she'd turn and—

He must have made a noise because, startled, Casey jumped and turned to face him. "Holy—"

Michael blinked, torn out of his fantasy. "You'd better not be about to curse," he said, smiling at her. She looked flushed and flustered. Her eyes widened with surprise at first but narrowed after she considered his comment.

"I was about to say 'holy cow.'"

He nodded, watching her closely. What was it

about this social worker that drove his libido crazy? Normally, he wouldn't give a woman like Casey a second look. She wasn't even remotely his type.

But maybe that was the problem. He'd been working so much he hadn't dated in a while. Rather than having daydreams about this woman, he needed to call one of his regular dates. Jenny was always fun. Or maybe Denise.

Anyone but the redhead in front of him.

"So, did you finish all your calls?" she asked, turning slightly.

She was no less attractive in profile, he decided.

"I made a few. I got you another four hundred."

Casey stopped in mid-motion, turned her head, and rewarded him with a tiny smile. Or maybe it wasn't a smile. Her lips lifted a fraction of an inch. But at least it wasn't a frown.

"That's nice. I appreciate it," she said.

He nodded absently as she turned back to her task. The lady didn't like him. Not one bit. And here he'd taken the plunge and navigated his way across the main room just to speak to her.

He cleared his throat. "It was no problem."

She pushed her hair away from her forehead, then turned to face him, wearing a distracted expression. "I'm sorry. What were you saying?"

"What's wrong with those plates?"

"We're two lunches short," she said. "I don't know how this keeps happening, but it does."

He glanced over his shoulder at the seniors in the main room, then back over at Casey.

"So just have whoever brings these things, bring some more."

"They won't come back today," Casey said. "These meals have to be ordered twenty-four hours in advance. I'll have to whip something up. Unfortunately, we don't keep much food here, but whatever I come up with is better than asking two people to forego their hot lunch."

Now she was in his territory. Problem-solving was his life's blood. He grinned, oddly pleased he could help.

"Hold on a second," he said. "What are the rest of the people having?"

She regarded him with open suspicion, but she answered anyway. "Meatloaf, mashed potatoes, green beans, and pudding."

"If I can use your phone again, I can solve this." She moved toward him, her hands on her hips. "How?"

"I'll just call the cafeteria at Barret Software and tell them to send over some extra lunches."

"And they'll do it?" Casey asked.

"Sure."

"Great! Then do it, and after that, I guess your two hours today are done. Tomorrow, I'd like you to help with some repairs around the center." She hesitated a moment, then said, "Thanks."

With that, she brushed by him and headed out of

the kitchen. But Michael had caught her expression before she'd walked away. She was surprised by his offer. Apparently, she hadn't expected him to help.

Feeling inordinately pleased with himself, Michael headed across the room to use Casey's phone. The woman mystified him. No doubt about it, she liked to be a helper. She probably wanted to have her hands in making the world better. Most people just wrote a check, but not her.

Was that why she was here? It had to be, because without even trying, she could be a big success working for a company like Barrett Software. She projected a great image, managed resources well, and obviously knew how to hold her own in an argument.

Something she'd said finally hit him. Tomorrow she wanted him to do repairs around the center. Him? Repairs? Yeah, that wasn't going to work.

He glanced around but didn't see Casey. Well, he didn't have time to discuss this with her right now, but tomorrow he'd set her straight. There was no way he could do repairs. He was mechanically challenged. Hopelessly inept at things like that.

No way was he doing repairs.

No way.

$\mathscr{H}$ 4 $\mathscr{H}$

I f today wasn't the worst day of her life, it ranked right up there in the top five. Sure, there had been prom night when she'd turned out to be allergic to her corsage and spent most of the night with her nose running like Niagara Falls.

And yeah, she had spoken at a city council meeting and found out later her slip was showing. But today was still pretty bad. Her feet ached; her head hurt, and she wanted Michael Parker out of her life.

Groaning, she trudged up the stairs to her small apartment, her groceries in imminent danger of tumbling out of the overstuffed bag. With effort, she shoved open the door to her apartment and headed to the kitchen.

No two ways about it, Michael Parker stumped her. How could he live the way he did, always chasing promotions and raises? How could he feel fulfilled by just a job, especially one that didn't help people?

Her father used to say the best way to help other people was to help yourself. But Casey didn't buy his theory. She couldn't stand the thought of not working directly on a cause she believed in.

The seniors at the center made her feel wanted and welcomed, and she knew she made a difference. Each time she improved the program, she had a positive effect, and as far as she was concerned, that was all that mattered in life.

The cross-stitched adage hanging in her grandmother's living room had read: When I Go, I'm Taking My Memories with Me. That was what Casey wanted— memories, a lot of them, of smiles and laughs, hugs and kisses.

After she put the last can of chicken noodle soup away, she tucked her canvas shopping bag in the cabinet and sat at the oak kitchen table.

How in the world could she come up with fifty thousand in just a few weeks? She'd have a better chance flying by flapping her arms. Still, she had to find a way. The seniors were depending on her.

Like a flash from a camera, an idea flared in her mind. Of course. A fundraiser. It was the only way, especially since she was down to just twenty-six days to raise the money. Sure, putting together an activity that big in such a short time would take something close to a miracle, but what choice did she have?

The center could invite the citizens of Honey, and the seniors could decide what sort of fundraiser it should be. Then she'd move heaven and earth to make sure it happened.

She smiled. Now this was something Michael could really help with. Working at a major corporation had to have taught him how to pull together a huge project. He could also invite all his business associates and all of the Barrett Software employees. Heck, he could probably stock the fundraiser with just the people he knew.

Suddenly, Casey felt very satisfied with herself. Her father had always maintained she didn't have a businesswoman's mind. Boy, was he ever wrong. She was about to prove she could multitask with the best of them.

"Nathan, I need to talk to you." Michael moved farther into his boss' office, carefully stepping over some errant golf balls.

It was a little past ten in the morning, a time that Nathan called the midmorning break. All employees were encouraged to de-stress for fifteen minutes, but personally, Michael called it a waste of time. He didn't need to take a fifteen-minute break every couple of hours. His mind stayed sharp no matter how long he worked.

Nathan putted and then hooted when the ball went into an overturned plastic cup. "Man, I'm good. You need to take up golf, Michael. It clears the mind.

Helps you sort things out."

Michael frowned and refrained from pointing out to his boss that he wasn't exactly playing at Pebble Beach. "No, thanks. My mind is clear enough."

"Suit yourself. But if you want to succeed in business, you have to take care of yourself. You don't want to burn out."

Michael dropped into one of the leather chairs. "I work out, which keeps me healthy."

Nathan raised one eyebrow and gave Michael a pointed look. "Healthy in body, but not in spirit."

Michael was starting to have second thoughts about taking this job. It was an excellent company and looked great on his resume, but Nathan was way too focused on happiness for his liking. It was annoying and playing havoc with Michael's life.

"I think my spirit's in good shape, too." Michael impatiently watched Nathan make two more putts, both landing directly in the cup.

"I'm amazing," Nathan said, smiling. "Wait until I tell my brothers."

Trying to show interest, Michael asked, "So they play golf?"

Nathan laughed. "No. It's just that we compete at everything." He placed the putter against his desk and returned to the large leather chair behind it. "What can I do for you?"

"Nathan, this volunteer work is impossible." Michael leaned forward, anxious to impress the seriousness of this situation on his boss. "Your managers all put in two hours yesterday at the charities. We can't afford to miss so much time from work."

When he finished speaking, Michael leaned back. Tension ran through his blood like a toxin. He desperately wanted to change Nathan's mind. Seldom had he believed in something so strongly as he did in this. Nathan was wrong. Pure and simple. Sure, in a perfect world, everyone would have time to volunteer for worthy causes. And he had to admit, what he'd seen yesterday had shown him the Honey Senior Citizen Center was a worthy cause.

But the senior executives of Barrett Software were the wrong ones to be helping out. They needed to be at their desks, doing their jobs, building a stronger company. Stronger companies made a stronger city, which helped everyone.

Just looking at Nathan, though, didn't give Michael much hope. His face had a resigned look to it.

"Michael, I know this seems like a lot to ask, but in the long run, helping others always helps oneself."

And a bird in the hand makes a mess on your palm.

"In this competitive market, Barrett Software needs to maximize its resources," Michael argued. "We need all our employees working at their full potentials at all times."

Nathan slowly shook his head. "Studies have shown companies with strong ties to their communities do better."

The tension in Michael grew to epic proportions. How could Nathan, an incredibly intelligent man, not see he could ruin a great company? Michael ran through possible arguments in his mind, studying the other man closely. There had to be a way to make him see reason.

"Why don't we just make some sizable donations to the charities? I think cash would help them more. For instance, the Honey Senior Citizen Center you assigned me to needs money for a new building. I can guarantee you the director would prefer you give her a big, fat check rather than send me down there every day. I'm in her way," he added. "She doesn't like it."

A wide grin graced Nathan's face and did nothing to settle Michael's nerves. "Glad to hear you're fitting in so well," he said with a laugh. "When they gave me the list of local charities needing help, I knew the Honey Senior Citizen Center was the right place for you."

A niggling suspicion ran up Michael's spine. "And why was that, Nathan?"

Nathan scratched the side of his neck and avoided Michael's gaze. "Oh, this and that."

Michael silently counted to ten. Then to twenty. Then gave up. One look at the self-satisfied face of his boss told him he was wasting his time. And time was a short commodity in his life these days.

"Are you going to reconsider this?" Michael asked, already knowing the answer.

"I'll make you a deal." Nathan rose and picked up

his putter. "I won't always expect everyone to donate ten hours a week, but I want my executive team to do it for at least a couple of months. At the end of that time, we'll talk."

For the first time since the memo had reached his desk, Michael saw a glimmer of hope. He stood and tucked his hands in his pockets. "Great."

Nathan toed a golf ball into place, studied it for a second, then tipped his head and looked at Michael. "If that place needs money, I expect you to help them raise it."

"Why don't we just—"

"Raise it, Michael. Don't give it to them. People need your time more than they need your money." Nathan's gaze didn't waver. "Keep that in mind."

Michael studied the wooden shelf in his hand, then eyed the wall in front of him. How hard could it be to hang one tiny shelf? He could do this. Hanging a shelf wasn't like making repairs. Not really. After all, driving a couple of nails into the wall wasn't like performing brain surgery. He could do this. No sweat.

Just like he could pull off this volunteer gig for a few months. Sure, it would be difficult, but like they said at Barret Software—Find A Way.

That was his life philosophy. When faced with a negative situation he flat out couldn't change, he found a way to turn it into a positive. The center was just such a situation, and he'd find a way to turn this negative to a positive.

Rummaging through the toolbox Casey had left him, he picked out a couple of nails. This would have been easier if Casey were here. But she was out picking up supplies and had left him a note asking him to work on the shelf. Still, he could do this, so he chose a spot and drove in the first nail. With only a tap, it flattened against the plasterboard.

"You need a molly."

Michael turned to find Al Terford standing behind him.

"Excuse me?"

Al chuckled and moved forward. "That nail won't hold squat if you don't anchor it. You need a molly."

"Who's Molly?"

"It's a piece of hardware, not a woman." Al chuckled again and dug around in the toolbox. "There aren't any in here. Tell you what. You pull that nail out of the wall while I go look in the supply cabinet and see if we have some mollies lying around."

Michael sighed. Of course he needed a molly. There was a good chance he could use a lobotomy, too, if they had one in the supply cabinet. Michael turned the hammer around. Maybe this wasn't as easy as he'd first thought. Well, he'd just pull the nail out of the wall, then ask Al to help him with the shelf. He had an M.B.A., for God's sake. What did he know about hanging a shelf?

LORI WILDE & LIZ ALVIN

The bottom line was, he should be at the office, not here playing Randy the Repairman for some kindhearted beauty. He pushed down the stress brewing inside him and forced himself to turn his thoughts back to the positive. There had to be an upside to being at the center.

An image of Casey automatically flashed into his mind like an unwanted response to an inkblot test. He immediately dismissed the thought. Whatever Casey Richards was, she wasn't a positive in this equation. She was a distraction, a highly attractive distraction, but a distraction nonetheless.

However, Nathan's appreciation of his work for the center was a positive. If Michael made Nathan happy, then he would probably follow his recommendation on the merger.

Granted, Michael would have to work his butt off over the next couple of months to keep up with things at the office while still managing to make a significant contribution at the center. But he could do it. He didn't believe in half efforts. He'd seen his old man give up too many times to ever let that type of failure touch him.

With effort, he tried to push aside the errant, long-buried image of his father. Michael never thought about Burt Parker. Never. But that was what Casey and this place did to him. They made him think all sorts of crazy thoughts. Thoughts about his job. About his life.

About his father. It didn't take a psychologist to

52

figure it out. Casey was disappointed in him; something that hadn't happened to him in years. Hadn't happened since the last time he'd spoken to his father.

If only Burt Parker could see him now. Here he was, an executive at Barrett Software, trying to hang a dumb shelf. His father had told him time and again to blow off college and take up a trade. That way, he could just work when the spirit struck him. But unlike his old man, Michael didn't mind hard work.

And he hadn't failed at anything since he'd left his family's ranch when he'd turned eighteen. No way was he about to start now. One way or the other, he would make this volunteer stint work. He wasn't going down in flames, no matter how hot it might feel at the moment.

"Hold on, Casey Richards," he muttered. "I'm going to make some real changes around this place."

Using the claw part of the hammer, he tried to get the nail out of the wall. It took a couple of attempts, but eventually, he grabbed the nail and pulled. Hard.

A hole the size of his head appeared.

Casey looked at the hole in the wall, then glanced at Michael. He gave her what could only be called a sheepish grin.

"Sorry about that, but I'm not really good at repairs."

"So I see," she said, not sure whether to laugh or cry.

"A dab of wood dough will fix that," Al offered.

"Are you kidding? My dog could fit through that hole."

Casey recognized the last speaker as Dottie. She bit back her own amazement at the mess Michael had made and turned to face the group.

"It's not so bad," she made herself say. "We'll get it fixed."

Before a huge discussion could break out, Casey headed to her office. She should have realized Michael wasn't the repair type. But hey? How hard was it to hang one simple shelf? Sheesh.

"I really do feel bad about the hole," Michael said. He'd followed her to her office. Now he came inside and shut the door. "I'll pay for the repairs."

Casey shook her head. "Don't worry about it. I can probably fix it; I'm good at fixing things."

He dropped into the chair facing her desk. "Well, apparently, I have a real affinity for breaking things."

"So I'm noticing." She sat in her own chair and studied him. She still couldn't get used to how handsome Michael was. He was far too handsome for her own good. And the little bit of embarrassment still clinging to him only made him look cuter. Which was dangerous. Very dangerous.

Shifting her thoughts away from that Pandora's box, she forced herself to focus on the problem at hand. "I thought things over last night, and I've decided we're going about this all wrong."

"Going about what?" he asked absently, flicking plaster off his designer slacks.

"The donations. We need a lot of money quickly. To do that, we need to schedule some sort of major fundraiser."

Michael looked at her and frowned. "That sounds like a huge effort. What about the money I raised for you yesterday?"

"It's great. Don't get me wrong. But unless you go on a swearing streak and end up giving me several thousand, we won't have enough." She waited, hoping he'd rise to the idea. Instead, he only frowned more.

"Do you have any experience with fundraisers?" he asked.

She refused to let him dampen her enthusiasm. "No. But I'm a quick learner, and I'm sure the seniors have a lot of ideas." She smiled. "Plus, rumor has it you're good at managing things."

He finally returned her smile. "Some people don't consider that a positive."

Michael was teasing her, and she had to admit, he was appealing like this, relaxed and joking. "On further consideration, some people have decided your talent can be very helpful."

"So, what's in it for you if you raise this money?" he asked. "Will you get promoted?"

Scratch that appealing thought. The shark had sprung a giant dorsal fin. "It's not like that. Forget I brought the idea up. I should have known you wouldn't understand."

"Ah, hell, Casey—"

She glared at him. "One dollar."

He chuckled. "Okay. Maybe I'll learn. Eventually."

She didn't share his humor. "I'm starting to have my doubts."

"Look, Casey, I didn't mean that the way it sounded. I just think a fundraiser sounds like a lot of extra work for you, especially if you aren't going to get anything out of it."

She leaned forward, placing her arms on the battered desk. "Not everything in the world revolves around the bottom line."

"Sure it does. Everyone wants something. It's human nature."

Disappointment washed through her at his statement. But what had she expected? Once a shark, always a shark.

Slowly, she studied him, taking her time. Michael never looked away. She knew she'd surprised him again. No doubt very few people could maintain eye contact with Michael Parker for long. But Casey never flinched. And after half a minute, she felt something new enter the equation. Something potent.

Something sexual.

The sensation settled around them, dancing across the room, making her skin tingle. Stunned, she blinked and broke eye contact, but the feeling didn't dissipate as expected. Instead, it became more noticeable. The air in the room felt thick, heavy with awareness. Loaded with anticipation.

She glanced back at Michael. It was obvious he felt it, too. He sat board-straight in his chair, a half-chagrined, half-amazed look on his face.

They both spoke at the same time.

"Um, I guess—"

"Casey, why don't—"

They stopped talking and stared at each other. Sure, from time to time she'd meet a man who interested her. In those cases, if he was nice, she'd go out with him. But if he was in any way the wrong type, she'd just dismiss the feeling; and that was that. No two ways about it, Michael was the wrong type with a capital *W*.

Unfortunately, she knew it wouldn't be that easy to ignore Michael. He was too intense. Too compelling.

Too sexy.

Shoot. As if her life wasn't already complicated enough, now why'd this have to happen?

❧ 5 ❧

Michael sat staring at Casey, wondering what in the world had gone on here. One minute he'd been arguing with her, then the next thing he'd known, everything had changed. Of all the times to act like a teenager. He needed to get a grip on himself before he lost it completely.

After a few tense moments, he said, "You were telling me about the fundraiser."

Casey fiddled with a red pencil on her desk. "Right. The fundraiser. I haven't come up with any ideas yet, but I'm sure the seniors can think of something."

"You're going to ask the people here what they think you should do? That'll take a lot of time." The soft, hazy look on her face evaporated like mist under a hot sun. Drat. He'd ticked her off again.

"The fundraiser is for their new facility. Of course, I'm asking them what they'd like to do." She leaned back in her chair. "I'm still not sure this is the right place for you. You seem so reluctant to get involved with the people. Yesterday, you hardly stepped out of the office at all."

Hey, he didn't deserve that. Okay, so he hadn't mingled. He wasn't a mingler by nature. But he'd been involved. He'd raised money. And he'd talked to Al. And to those two women, Dottie and Elmira. He hadn't hidden.

"I stepped out when I arranged for the extra lunches to be brought over," he pointed out, then felt more than a little childish for doing so.

The glimmer in her eyes faded a tad. "Right. Thanks."

He'd seldom heard "thank you" said with less sincerity. Hard to imagine that just moments ago, the air in here had crackled with sexual tension. Right now, Casey Richards looked as if she wanted to toss him out on his butt and lock the door behind him.

Which would suit him just fine.

"So, see, I mingled," he said. At her dubious look, he added, "Okay. Maybe not a lot. I'll do better."

He could practically see the gears in her head turning. He knew she wanted to get rid of him. But since she hadn't yet, he was willing to bet she didn't have any more choice in his being here than he did. She depended on volunteer organizations for personnel and finances. Chances were, she couldn't just pick and choose who she wanted.

Just like he couldn't walk away unless he wanted

to risk his job. Whatever other differences separated them, maybe they were tied together in some sort of crazy way.

Lord, he hoped not. Working here felt like being in a maze. Every time he turned a corner, he thought he'd found the way out of this problem. Then he realized he'd simply run into another dead end.

A couple of months. Nathan had said this crazy scheme could be renegotiated after a couple of months. Forty workdays at the most, two hours a day. He could do that. Heck, he'd already made it through yesterday.

He only had thirty-nine days left. A new thought hit him.

"When do you need this money for the modifications?" Maybe, just maybe, luck would be with him, and she wouldn't hold this fundraiser for a few months. He'd be long gone by then.

"I've only got twenty-six days left if we want to get the house. The owners were willing to hold it for us for a month. If we can't work out the finances, it will go on the market. Someone will snap it up in a second."

"How much money do you need?"

When she paused, he knew he wasn't going to like her answer. "Fifty thousand dollars."

Michael pushed out of his chair. "You're kidding, right? No way can you pull off a fundraiser that big in such a short amount of time. Why didn't you start raising this money sooner? Casey, dammit—"

Casey looked furious. He knew he wasn't helping things, but instinct told him he was better off if Casey Richards kept disliking him. When she silently held out her hand, he groaned.

"I know. One dollar," he said. Before she could say anything, he pulled his wallet out of his inside jacket pocket, withdrew a five-dollar bill, and placed it in her hand. "I'm sure I'll owe you more than that before the afternoon is over."

She rose. "No, you won't. I told you yesterday to stop cursing here." Placing both hands on her desk, she ignored the slight wobble and stared at him.

"If it's any of your business, I didn't know I needed this money until two days ago," she continued. "The city originally told me they would cover all the costs. But then they reexamined the budget and found out they didn't have enough money. One of the councilmen called me at five o'clock the day before last and told me. You showed up yesterday. So, as you can see, I started working on the problem as soon as I could."

He hated to rock her boat, but as far as he could tell, it was already sinking, so what the hell. "No way can you put together a major event in a few weeks. There are too many details to take care of."

"I will make this happen." She spoke slowly, clearly. Although the volume of her voice never changed, the impact of her words did. He didn't doubt for a moment that she believed what she said. "And I'll do it without your help."

LORI WILDE & LIZ ALVIN

"Fine."

"Good." She nodded her head in the direction of the door. "Since I'm going to be busy making plans, you can't work in my office today. Please go join the seniors. Several of the groups are playing pinochle. You can play, too."

Pinochle? He swallowed past the tense knot in his throat. "I don't know how to play."

"They can teach you."

Then she smiled. Well, sort of smiled. Her lips pulled back, and he could see her teeth. But then again, you could see a mad dog's teeth right before he attacked. Michael shifted, uncertain how to act in this situation. It had been years since anyone had shoved him around like this. And even then, he'd only put up with it because he wanted to get ahead. Like he wanted to get ahead now. "Pinochle isn't really my style," he said.

Her fake smile didn't waver, but he could read anger in her eyes. He was fairly certain she didn't like him. Which was a shame because he had to admit, he liked her a lot. Maybe too much. She had grit, even if she had chosen to waste her time working at a dead-end job. Casey also surprised him. Her personality didn't suit her soft, somewhat romantic looks.

He watched, fascinated, as she leaned forward and said, "Then change your style."

Casey watched Michael leave her office, wishing a giant anvil would land on his head. She should have expected him to balk at helping. In a way, she didn't blame him. They really didn't stand much chance of raising the money in such a short time. But she didn't want to admit that, even to herself. As long as even a few hours remained, she had to try.

Sighing, she leaned back in her chair, ignoring the woeful creak the worn metal made. Okay, so if she was going to do this, she needed to get moving. This afternoon, she could poll the seniors for ideas. She glanced at her calendar. The fundraiser would have to be the last Saturday of the month. That gave her twenty-four days.

She knew it was a long shot, but then again, so many things in life were. Even her parents—who hated what she did for a living—would admire her for trying to pull off the impossible. Her father always said that nothing got the adrenaline pumping like accomplishing the impossible. And that's what she would do. She'd reach down inside herself, find a little magic, and get everything she wanted. All of it.

"You're either an incredible optimist or an incredible fool," she muttered to herself. She rose and headed toward the main room to survey the seniors for fundraiser ideas. What was that saying? The only difference between a visionary and a madman was the advertising campaign.

She'd just have to make certain she had a terrific campaign.

❧

"Mind if I join you?" Michael asked Al and another man who were seated at the table farthest from Casey's office. The pair looked engrossed, so he figured he could sit for a while without them bothering him. Then in a half hour or so, he could go back and talk to Casey again. Maybe apologize.

Al looked up from his cards. "Have a seat."

Michael introduced himself to the other man, who shook his hand with a surprisingly firm grip.

"I'm Tommy Gilbert," the man said. "Nice hole you put in the wall."

Michael nodded. "Yeah. I try my best."

Both older men turned their attention back to their cards, and Michael pulled up a chair. For several minutes, he just sat quietly. Then he noticed Casey come into the room. He watched her move from person to person, speaking to each one. Her smile now was natural, making her even prettier than usual.

"She's a heck of a lady."

Michael turned and met the amused gaze of Tommy Gilbert.

"Yes. She is."

Tommy's brown eyes twinkled. "Not bad-looking, either. If I were thirty years younger, I'd—"

"Still be too old for her," Al interjected. He chuckled for a moment at his own joke, then added, "Besides, even if you were her age, she wouldn't go out with you."

He tipped his head down and looked at Michael over the top of his glasses. "She hasn't agreed to go out with you, has she?"

The question caught Michael off guard. "I haven't asked her out," he said.

Tommy snorted. "Coward. Don't you know that you can't be shy around women? You need to ask 'em out before some other guy comes along and gets them first."

"Like you know anything about women," Al said. "You can't get Elmira to go out with you."

"Well, you haven't had any luck, either. And you've asked her a lot more than I have."

Michael relaxed a little, thinking that maybe the men had forgotten about him. But before long, they had exhausted their critique of each other's style and turned to study him.

"You do like women, don't you?"

Michael blinked. "Yes."

Tommy wagged a finger at him. "Then you need to get moving. I don't know how Casey's slipped by this long, but I'm sure sooner or later some lucky fella will come along and nab her. She'll make a great wife."

Al made a snorting noise again. "Women aren't like that anymore. Don't you watch TV? Women have careers. They don't need to marry anymore."

Tommy leaned forward. "I didn't say she needed to get married. But a lady like Casey will fall in love. Then she'll want to get married."

"He'd better be special because she sure is," Al said.

Michael nodded absently and glanced back at Casey. The men were right—she was special. But too soft. Too involved. She was a broken heart waiting to happen.

Or maybe it had happened already. Maybe that was why she wasn't married. Or maybe she just spent too much time worrying about this place. He still couldn't believe she expected to raise all that money in under a month. She could never do it. But he admired her for trying.

"So, you want to play?" Al asked, indicating the cards in his hand.

"No. I don't play pinochle."

Tommy and Al laughed. "Well, that's not exactly what we're playing."

Michael pulled his gaze away from Casey and looked at the men. "No?"

"No. It's just a friendly game of poker," Al said. Michael was prepared to say yes when the door opened and Drew Charlin, a Honey council member, walked in. Michael knew the man and had attended a meeting where he'd been present. Tall, with blond hair and a polished manner, Drew was a natural politician.

Drew Charlin didn't notice Michael when he flashed a smile at the crowd. He stopped next to Casey and bent over to say something to her. The sight annoyed Michael, so he forced himself to look away. What did he care if Casey was friends with the council member? They probably dated. It was none of his business.

Still, he had to exert a lot of self-control when he glanced back and saw Casey rise and lead the way to her office. When Drew shut the door behind them, Michael muttered a curse.

"I'll second that," Tommy said, tossing a dollar bill on the table. "Can't stand the man. He's not right for her."

Michael couldn't stop himself from asking, "Do they date?"

"Not as far as I know, but he's always coming here and asking her out." Al carefully removed one dollar from his wallet and then proudly denounced Drew Charlin's parentage. "A man ought to know when to leave a woman alone."

Michael refrained from pointing out that both Tommy and Al had asked Elmira out several times. Instead, he nodded. The thought of Casey with Drew bothered him way too much to be good for his own well-being.

"What do you mean that the city may withdraw the funding for the new center?" Casey asked, pacing her small office. "You've committed that money to us."

Drew shrugged his elegantly clad shoulders. "I know, but some of the council feel the money could be better spent elsewhere. Believe me, I'm trying everything I can to put in a good word for you, Casey. But let's face it—no one believes you can raise the money for the modifications. And if you fail, then the center might as well renew the lease here."

"But this building is falling apart, and it's too small."

"I'm sorry. The city just doesn't have enough money. If you can't come up with your share, then there's nothing we can do to help you."

Casey sucked in a tight breath. There was no sense arguing with Drew. If the city had the money, she knew he would help her. But the money didn't exist unless she raised it.

"Drew, tell the council to wait until the end of the month. I will have the money. I promise you."

Drew rose and smoothed his jacket into place. "You need to face facts—you can't do this. You're just one person. You can't raise all that money without any help. And as much as I'd like to help, at the moment—"

"I have help."

His look was dubious. "What help?"

"The seniors."

"I don't think so," Drew said, standing and laughing softly. When she frowned at him, he choked back the sound. "Sorry. Anyway, I wish you luck. But I did have another reason for stopping by. I also was wondering if you'd go to dinner with me on Friday." He opened the office door.

She'd rather dip herself in honey and sit on an anthill, but the council wavering wasn't Drew's fault. He was nice enough, but he didn't get her pulse racing. "I can't."

Without meaning to, she glanced out her office and studied a group of men playing cards at a corner table, her gaze landing on Michael Parker. When she felt her heart rate increase, she silently groaned. Now, why couldn't Drew have that same effect on her? Why did she have to be attracted to a shark?

Sheesh. She was a sad and sorry case.

Thoroughly exhausted by the time he left his office at eight, Michael unlocked his Mercedes and opened the door. He couldn't believe he still had to meet with a potential merger candidate tonight. The company owner had insisted they meet for dinner, and by the time they finished, he'd be too tired to move.

No way could he keep this pace up. He couldn't spend a large part of each day at the center, then work a full day at the office. And today, all he'd done at the center—well, besides make the hole in the wall —was play cards. After Drew left, Casey had remained shut up in her office.

She'd invited several of the seniors in to talk to her, but she hadn't invited him. He'd left without saying another word to her.

Fine. Let her ignore him. Life would be a lot simpler if he could get Casey out of his life and out of his mind. Several times this afternoon, he'd found himself thinking about her while in a meeting. The extra demand on his time was turning him loony.

Shrugging off his jacket, he went to set it on the passenger seat Oddly, it felt lighter than usual. He patted the pockets, searching for his cell phone and came up empty-handed.

"Ah, hell," he said when he remembered he'd left it at the center. He'd had his jacket off all afternoon and hadn't noticed it missing. Slipping behind the wheel of his car, he considered his options. The smart thing to do was to forget the phone and head on to the restaurant. The center would be closed by now.

But he wanted his phone. Crazy as it seemed, he felt naked without it. One of his girlfriends had once said he was a control freak and would probably cut off his own arm before he'd give up his cell phone. She hadn't been too far off. He didn't like being out of the loop. With his phone, he could stay on top of the million fires he had to deal with on a daily basis.

Funny how he hadn't noticed the phone missing before now. But that was what the center did to him. What Casey did to him. She drove him nuts. He never forgot things. He kept a running list of important tasks in his head at all times. And he'd never forgotten his phone.

Until Casey had thrown him into a tailspin. Without stopping to analyze his motives, he turned right out of the Barret Software parking lot and headed toward the center. Even if it was a long shot, he wanted to try to get his phone. Maybe then, he could get some control back in his life.

When he pulled up in front of the center, the outside lights were on, but it looked fairly dark inside. Michael glanced around. A compact car sat in the far corner of the parking lot, but it could have been left overnight. Michael walked to the front door and knocked, not really expecting an answer. But seconds later, the door flew open, and Casey stood on the other side. Except she didn't look like the Casey he knew. Her hair was a mess; she had smears of dirt on her face, and the front of her T-shirt was wet.

"What the hell happened to you?" Michael asked. Before she could answer, he moved past her.

Casey shut and locked the door behind him. "Look, I don't know why you're here, but I'm busy. So when you finish cursing, leave the money on my desk."

She turned and headed in the direction of the kitchen, with Michael right on her heels. "Seriously, what's wrong?"

Casey entered the kitchen and then moved aside so he could see.

"The pipe under the sink broke tonight. Thank goodness I was here to turn off the water. As you can see, it made quite a mess."

Michael scanned the situation. "A mess" was an understatement. Water was everywhere.

"Have you called a plumber?"

Casey tipped her head and regarded him through narrowed eyes. "Yes. He'll stop by tomorrow to fix the pipe." She knelt and mopped up water with a sponge. "Why are you here?"

"I forgot my cell phone," he muttered.

"It's in the top drawer of my desk. I found it this afternoon."

He nodded absently. "Can't this wait until tomorrow?"

Casey shook her head. She'd pulled her hair into a ponytail, no doubt to keep it from dragging in the water. "No. I need to mop this water up tonight before it damages the floor."

He glanced toward the door. He really had to go meet his colleague. But an unnerving thought hit him —only a lazy bum like his dad would leave Casey stranded with this mess. His decision made, Michael headed out the door. When he reached his car, he got his workout clothes from the trunk. If he was going to spend the next couple of hours crawling on the floor, he wasn't going to do it in an Armani suit.

6

Casey watched Michael walk away. Figured. Of course he'd leave her with this mess. He'd probably grab his expensive phone and hightail it home. A hotshot executive like him wouldn't think twice about deserting her.

Exasperated, she continued to sop up water, twisting the sponge roughly over the bucket. After another few minutes passed, she'd still barely made a dent. At this rate, she'd be here most of the night. She heard the front door open again, then footsteps.

For a second, she thought Michael might have come back to help her. Instead, he walked in the opposite direction toward her office and the restrooms. Peachy-keen great. Thank goodness she'd been here tonight so he could get his phone back and use the bathroom.

Casey wiped a weary hand across her forehead, pushing back some stray strands of hair drooping in her eyes. If only Michael had offered to help. She might've had a chance at finishing in time to go home and get a few hours of sleep.

"What did you expect?" she muttered, wringing the sponge into the bucket and wishing it were his corporate shark neck.

A few minutes later, she heard the sound of foot-steps approaching the kitchen. Casey spun around, barely preventing herself from slipping on the wet floor, and froze. Before her stood an amazing sight. Not only had Michael returned, but he'd changed his clothes. Casey rose slowly to her feet, wiping her wet hands on her jeans. Instead of a designer suit, Michael wore a faded red T-shirt and shorts.

He looked different. Less formal. Less forceful, but equally dangerous. Casey swallowed past a lump in her throat the size of a grapefruit. The man was gorgeous. She'd always thought he was handsome. But now he was a lonely lady's midnight dream and far too good-looking to be alone with.

"Thanks for understanding, Ted," Michael was saying into his cell phone, finally it was working. "How about we meet tomorrow? What time works for you?" After a moment, he said, "Great. See you then."

Michael pushed the Off button on his phone, then looked at Casey. She narrowed her eyes. "Why did you come back?"

"To help." He set his phone down on the counter. "Don't you have a mop?"

"We did, but I can't seem to find it." Stunned, she continued to stare at him. Had she heard right? Did he just cancel a meeting to help her mop the floor?

"Your appointment sounded important."

Michael shrugged. "Ted's a good guy. He was happy to reschedule."

Warmth pervaded her at his words. Wow. He'd canceled his meeting. Would wonders never cease?

Michael headed toward the supply cabinet, slipping a little on the wet floor. With a chuckle and a grin to Casey, he deliberately slid across the room, stopping himself by bumping lightly against the cabinet.

"Don't I remind you of Tom Cruise in his underwear?" He shot her another killer grin.

"Um. I guess." Casey felt her heart rate kick into overdrive. Oh, no. Michael was much, much cuter than Tom Cruise. Unable to stop herself, her gaze skimmed down his body, landing finally on his feet. They were bare like her own. Even his feet were attractive. It seemed so intimate to be looking at his bare feet, so personal. With effort, she pulled her gaze away and looked at his face.

Michael met and held her gaze, the single bulb from the overhead light throwing his face partly into shadow. She felt his look like a touch as it skimmed her body. Her breathing increased. Sheesh. She needed to get out more. She was acting like a dieter in a chocolate factory. Avoiding his gaze, she knelt and started sopping up water again. "You don't have to help."

A second later, he knelt next to her, a matching sponge in his hand. "Sure, I do. I know you don't think much of me, but I wouldn't leave you alone with this mess."

Knowing it was risky but unable to stop herself, Casey turned her head so she could study him. This was a new and totally unexpected side to him. She would have expected him to pull out his checkbook and offer to pay someone to clean up. Anything but get down on his knees and help.

As if feeling her gaze, he stopped.

"What?" he asked softly, a quizzical smile gracing his handsome face.

"I'm surprised you came back," she admitted, finding it difficult to concentrate when he was watching her with those hypnotic blue eyes of his.

"Even ogres have their moments." He broke eye contact and went back to work.

"You're not an ogre," Casey said, amazed that she actually meant it.

His dry chuckle let her know he doubted her. "You didn't think so earlier today. In fact, I bet you definitely considered me top ogre."

A smile tugged at her lips. "Maybe not top ogre..." He raised an eyebrow, and she laughed. "But possibly vice ogre."

The humor on his face faded, and his expression turned thoughtful. "Sorry. I didn't mean to offend you about your chances of raising that money in time."

Casey twisted the sponge in her hand over the dented metal bucket and watched dirty water run through her fingers. "You didn't offend me, exactly—"

"Just really ticked you off."

She saw no point in denying the truth. "I don't like people telling me there's something I can't do."

"No one likes that."

"Exactly." She shifted so she faced him. "If only you understood—"

"Yeah, well, maybe I do. You know, there are things that are important to me, too."

Casey froze. Could the shark actually be human? "Like what?"

Michael hesitated, and Casey found herself holding her breath, willing him to tell her his thoughts. But he didn't. Instead, after long, agonizing moments, he shrugged.

"Did you get any ideas for your fundraiser?" he asked.

Well, drat. She sensed he'd been about to tell her something important about himself. Something she wanted to hear. But as much as Casey didn't want to let him change the subject, she understood people well enough to know when not to push.

"The seniors are thinking about it. I'm not sure any of the ideas I've gotten so far will work."

"Tell me about them."

Casey debated whether he was truly interested or

just humoring her. He seemed sincere, but still...
"Why? You don't think I can pull this off."

For a heartbeat of time, he just looked at her, and Casey felt the impact of his intent gaze. Then he shrugged. "I had no right to say that."

Warmth spread through Casey at his words. He was so different tonight, not at all like a boardroom bigwig. For starters, he'd admitted he'd made a mistake. Plus, now he was showing interest in her plans. How odd.

"Thank you for saying so," she said. "I'll admit it's a long shot, but—"

"You have to try." He nodded slowly, the light gleaming off his dark hair. "Yeah, I know."

"You'd try, too," Casey pointed out.

"Dam—" At her warning glance, he grinned and started over. "Sure. I love a challenge. So what were the ideas?"

"A walk-a-thon, a bazaar, and an auction—but rather than auctioning off items, the gentleman who suggested it thought we should auction off dates."

"You mean like those bachelor auctions?" Casey smiled, enjoying this conversation with Michael.

"Yes. He thought the ladies at the center might be willing to part with serious cash to have a romantic night on the town."

"You can't blame a guy for trying." He added a wink for emphasis, making Casey laugh. How could she ever have thought him stiff and unfriendly?

"Yeah, well, it might be the solution to his dating

problem, but I don't think it's the solution the center needs. But whatever we come up with, it has to be soon. I need to run the plans by the city council."

"You're a smart lady. You'll come up with something." His confidence in her caused an erratic fluttering in her stomach.

"Thanks."

"Once you decide, just tell the council this is what you're doing. Don't ask them," he said. "It's always easier to ask for forgiveness than for permission."

Michael's lopsided grin did funny things to Casey's metabolism. That grin invited her to share the joke, and she found she was smiling despite herself. She still couldn't believe he'd canceled a meeting to help. Michael was so approachable tonight he was impossible to resist. He genuinely seemed interested in what she had to say.

Which was a potent aphrodisiac.

As she continued to watch him, his eyes darkened, and his smile faded. Casey sucked in her breath on a hiss and felt a wave of desire hit her.

Who would have thought a man like Michael Parker would affect her this way? But here, now, in this quiet building on this lonely night, she couldn't remember ever finding a man as attractive as she found him.

Michael slowly set down his sponge, his heated gaze never leaving her face. With controlled, deliberate moves, he rose and extended his hand to her. Casey didn't have to ask what he was doing. She knew. Just like he knew. The air vibrated with the tension between them.

She took his hand, rose to her feet, and stood anxiously before him.

"This is a really bad idea," she said. But she made no move to resist when he placed his hands on her hips and pulled her forward until she pressed against him. This close, she could smell his tangy aftershave. He smelled like heaven, like temptation.

She was in big trouble.

"Yeah. I know." He kissed her neck, and she shivered. "Do you want me to stop?"

Casey pulled back just far enough to look at him.

She could see his desire, and she knew it mirrored her own. Desire born not of loneliness. Or fatigue. But of something stronger. Deeper. Certain now of her decision, she placed her hand on the side of his face and urged him forward.

"Hell, no," she murmured a second before her lips met his.

She expected Michael's kiss to be forceful, taking more than it gave. But rather, with tenderness, he brushed his lips against hers.

He moved with agonizing slowness from side to side. Reaching the corner of her lip, he nibbled softly, lingering just long enough to drive her wild. Then he moved on, seeking, searching. When he continued to coax her with teasing brushes, she realized he wanted her to show him just how far he could go.

His thoughtfulness touched her. Most men she'd

dated in recent memory kissed as if they were playing football. They turned a caress into a competition. But not Michael. Even though he no doubt possessed a keen killer instinct in business, he obviously understood that kissing was about pleasure, not conquest.

Tipping her head, she met his kiss more fully, wanting to savor the sensation. He made her feel not just desired but cherished. Michael slid his arms around her, cradling her body tightly against his own. The rhythm of the kiss made her pulse race with excitement A delicious ache settled on her, reminding her of how alone she'd been for so very long. This kiss was full of fire. And promise.

And magic.

Groaning, Michael cupped her face. Although his arms no longer held her, Casey felt herself pressing against his chest. In the back of her mind, she knew she stood in several inches of water in the battered kitchen of the center, kissing a man who was completely wrong for her. But she couldn't help it. This embrace felt right. This kiss felt right.

Eventually, reluctantly, she pulled her head back, separating their lips. For a moment, she expected him to protest. She could read the banked frustration on his face. Then he stepped back and moved away from her. Within the harsh light of the kitchen, she stared at him. His hands were knotted into fists at his sides. His face was taut, the muscles pulled tight.

And his eyes burned with the same fire she felt flickering through her veins.

"I didn't really intend that to happen," he finally said.

Casey nodded wordlessly, the reality of the situation overwhelming her. Michael Parker had kissed her. Holy cow. Worse yet, she'd kissed him back. Really kissed him. And she'd enjoyed it. Immensely. Immeasurably.

And she wanted to kiss him again.

"Aren't you going to say anything?" He had one dark eyebrow raised in question.

Great. Just what she wanted. A postmortem.

"What's there to say? We only kissed because it's late, and we're both tired." She moved past him and retrieved her sponge, ignoring the slight trembling in her hand. Talk about a dumb move. Kissing Michael ranked right up there with inviting a cannibal to brunch.

What had Elmira said? Men were like hats? Well, as far as Casey was concerned, she didn't need a hat, thank you very much. Even a hat that kissed as well as Michael did.

Kneeling, she resumed sopping up water, wanting to do anything but look at the man standing behind her. With uneven strokes, she rubbed the floor and squeezed the sponge into the bucket. The tingling on the back of her neck reminded her that Michael stood watching her.

What did he expect her to say? *Gee whiz, Mike, heck of a kiss you've got there?* What was the big deal? Okay, they'd kissed, whether they should have or not.

The downside was she could no longer look at him and see just the suit and the job. Not now, when she knew she desired Michael Parker and hated herself for that weakness.

"You owe the center a dollar," Michael said.

Casey stopped in mid-mop and glanced at him over her shoulder.

"I what?"

Michael crouched next to her, a teasing gleam in his eyes. "You cursed."

Casey blinked. What in the world was he talking about? She rarely cursed, only when... She gulped in a quick breath. He was right. She'd cursed. She turned back to her task, glad she no longer had to look at him.

"I did, so I'll pay," she said.

Michael moved to her side, picked up his sponge, and started wiping up water again. His movements were purposeful, his pace much faster than her own. Casey found herself watching his hands. The sure strokes. The wide swipes.

A bead of sweat trickled down her back. Suddenly, every move he made seemed seductive. His fingers flexed on the sponge, wringing the water into the pail. She couldn't help wondering how it would feel to have those same fingers caress her skin.

"I'll pay the dollar for you," he said, interrupting her thoughts.

Casey moved her gaze back to the sponge in her hand. Good grief. She'd just worked herself into a lather watching him wring out a sponge. Talk about being a basket case.

She forced herself to look at him. "I can pay for myself."

"No, really, I'd like to pay." Michael placed one hand on her arm, but when she jumped, he released her immediately. "What's wrong?"

Casey sighed. Why didn't he just let it go? She was going insane. That was the only logical explanation. "Drop it, Michael."

"But I really enjoyed that kiss, and it was worth a lot more than a dollar."

She half groaned, half laughed. What was with this man? Wasn't the male sex the one who hated to talk about things like kisses?

"Let it go," she repeated. "Let's finish with the floor."

Her gaze met his, and she felt the same fluttering sensation she'd felt when he'd kissed her. Of all the men in the world, why did it have to be Michael who pushed her On button?

"Casey, I'm as confused as you are. It's a bit like a dog finding out he's got a crush on a cat."

Absently, Casey smiled, but she had a sinking feeling a cat would fare better against a dog than she would fare with Michael. Suddenly, the mess of the floor seemed the least of her worries.

❧ 7 ❧

Michael sat in the meeting staring at the data projected on the screen. He hadn't a clue what he'd spent the last ten minutes looking at. All he'd been able to do was think about Casey. And last night. After the kiss, they'd finished wiping up the floor, annoyingly awkward with each other.

Talk about a stupid move. He hadn't even meant to kiss her, but once he had, he hadn't wanted to stop. She'd been soft and sweet and entirely too enticing in his arms. All sorts of great ideas had popped into his head.

But hey, he wasn't that stupid. He couldn't afford to get involved with Casey. Last night had shown him how easily he'd change work plans to be with her. If he didn't watch himself, he'd end up like some of the other managers—constantly having to choose between their personal life and work. No matter what decision those poor saps made, something ended up suffering.

But not him. Michael had figured out this rat maze as a kid. If you busted your butt and worked long and hard, you could make something out of yourself. Anything else was merely spitting in the wind. He'd spent his childhood living hand to mouth on a dirt ranch in the middle of nowhere. Never again. Now he was only one tiny step away from being part of a major merger. This was not the time to start thinking with his hormones rather than his head.

Gritting his teeth, he forced himself to concentrate on the meeting. The project was off-schedule, and the key personnel were presenting alternatives. Normally, he thrived on this kind of pressure. Nothing gave him a bigger rush than pulling off the impossible. But today it wasn't giving him the usual thrill.

Man, why had he gone and kissed Casey? That kiss could cause complications. Sure, last night she'd said the kiss didn't mean anything to her, but what if she'd changed her mind? Well, he'd just have to tell her when he saw her this afternoon that they could never kiss again. Last night had been an aberration. A simple matter of satisfying curiosity. But now they both knew what they needed to know, so that was that.

Michael sighed, wondering if he had any chance of getting Casey to buy that load of crap. He sure wasn't. The bottom line was he'd kissed Casey because he'd wanted to. But he wasn't about to let that kiss mess up his plans. There would be no repeats of last night. None. Ever.

⁂

"So what kind of responses did you get?" Elmira asked, entering Casey's office and sitting in the chair.

Casey thumbed through the papers she'd gotten this morning from the seniors and added them to the pile she'd gotten the previous day. "The new ideas are for a carnival, a casino night, a chili cook-off..." She lifted the last paper and laughed. "And a really big bake sale."

"Which one are we going to do?"

Casey placed the sheets of paper on her desk and smoothed the creases. "That's up to the group. I don't care, as long as it has the potential to make a lot of money. I'll wait one more day to see what other ideas come in."

Elmira regarded Casey with open curiosity. "Did you ask Michael what he thinks? He seems like a pretty smart guy."

The older woman's comment made the hair on the back of Casey's neck stand up. Her internal radar said Elmira was in here to do a little lobbying for Michael. Which was laughable. Michael was the last person to need help with anything. She'd learned last night how capable he was...at a lot of things.

"I've mentioned that the center plans on having a fundraiser." Casey studied the older woman and waited patiently for what she knew was coming. It didn't take long. Elmira patted her hair, flashed Casey a tentative smile, then leaned forward.

"Dear, the real reason I'm here is because Dottie and I have been talking, and we think..." She gave Casey a sweet smile. "We think you should ask Michael out."

Astonished, Casey stared at her. "Ask him out?"

"Yes. Women do it all the time, and we think you should ask him rather than waiting for him to ask you. You need to be assertive in today's dating market."

Casey bit back a smile. "Dating market?"

Elmira wagged one finger at Casey. "Don't make fun of me. I read the paper. I know how hard it is to find a good man these days. You have to remember, men are like fish."

"Fish? I thought they were like hats."

With a little tsking sound, Elmira said, "They're like fish. You can't let them know you're after them until you've caught them."

"But if I ask him out, he'll know I'm after him," Casey pointed out, more amused than annoyed by this latest matchmaking attempt.

"Casey, you ask him out, then once he's interested, you pretend you aren't."

Elmira delivered this advice slowly, as if she feared

Casey wouldn't understand it. Which, come to think of it, she didn't.

"Seems kind of manipulative to me," Casey said.

"No offense, but it isn't exactly as if your way is working. And you can't seriously want to spend your life alone. You need to get married and have your children before it's too late." Elmira leaned down and rooted through her large purse, which was sitting on the floor. When she straightened, she had a paperback book in her hand. "I borrowed this from one of my granddaughters. It has all sorts of suggestions you can use to land a fella."

She laid the book on the desk and pushed it toward Casey. The bright orange cover claimed the book contained surefire methods for seducing a man. Casey regarded it like a venomous snake. Gingerly, she nudged it back toward Elmira.

"Thanks, really. But I'm not interested in Michael that way," Casey said. She hated to lie, especially to Elmira, but in actuality, it wasn't a lie. Well, not completely. She wasn't interested in Michael, despite the kiss they'd shared. He was all wrong for her. Oh, he might have canceled one meeting, but he was still a man rooted to the fast track.

Now, in the light of day, she knew she must have been feeling weak last night. Yeah. That was it. She'd been so worried about the money that a fog had settled over her mind. And the kiss was just the result of too little sleep and an unexpectedly kind gesture from a handsome man.

Elmira rose, a serene smile gracing her face. She made no move to retrieve the paperback. "Keep the book just in case. You never know when you might change your mind. In my own case, it took me months before I'd even look at my husband. I never considered him the right sort for me." She tipped her head and regarded Casey over the top of her glasses. "Then one day, he pulled up in a shiny new car, and something magical happened. I saw him for what he really was."

"A good-looking man with a killer car?"

Elmira gave her one of those smug little looks she specialized in. "Amongst other things."

With that, she left Casey's office with her final words hanging in the air. Casey blew out a deep breath. Fine. Okay, so Elmira had been wrong, but she wasn't. Michael Parker really wasn't the right type for her. And last night had been one big, old fluke—a fluke that wouldn't happen again.

She had way too much at stake to risk it all on a case of lust, regardless of how strong that lust was. She needed to keep her mind sharp and her senses focused on raising the money for the center. If she didn't get a grip on herself soon, she'd end up pulling petals off flowers while saying, "He loves me, he loves me not."

"You are such a sap," she muttered. She picked up Elmira's book, intending on shifting it in her desk, when temptation got the better of her. Slowly, she flipped through the pages, stopping when she reached the chapter on how to make sex interesting. The warmth of a blush crept up her cheeks. When she reached a particularly erotic illustration, she slammed the book closed and shoved it in her desk drawer.

Still agitated, she glanced out her open office door into the main room. She could see Michael talking to Al and Tommy. Today he had on his usual shark uniform—expensive suit, expensive shirt, expensive tie. Darn his hide, he looked incredibly...tempting. Especially when images from that book were still lodged in her mind.

As he moved through the room, he surprised her by stopping and talking to a few more seniors on his way to her office. Apparently, he'd made a couple of friends yesterday afternoon. Drat. Lust she could fight, but he'd better not turn out to be a nice guy after all.

That would be way too much for her to take.

"Hi," Michael said, entering Casey's office cautiously. She looked flustered, which only made him curse himself more. Damn. What if she expected him to ask her out? He didn't want to hurt her feelings, but he also didn't want to mislead her. He sat in the chair across from her and debated how to approach this talk. He'd been less nervous firing errant employees than he was telling this woman he couldn't date her.

"Hi." Casey twiddled with a paper clip, her gaze skimming over him but not stopping. "Thanks for your help last night."

"No problem." He watched her mutilate the paper clip for a few seconds, then cleared his throat. "Casey, about last night—"

"Oh, yeah." She tossed the clip in the trash and flashed a too-bright smile at him. "We should just forget what happened."

"You mean the kiss?"

That too-bright smile seemed to stretch even wider. "Exactly."

Even though she was saying precisely what he'd planned on saying, she was strung like a tightrope. "I think that sounds like a good idea," he said slowly, trying to get her to meet his gaze.

She picked up another paper clip, and he pitied the tiny thing. "I mean, it was only a kiss. Certainly not the end of the world."

Soon, the twisted silver clip joined its mate in the trash. Michael shifted nervously in his chair. Was she upset they'd agreed to forget the kiss, or was she worried he might not be willing to let go of one of the best memories he'd had in years?

"Okay," he said. "But you seem kind of upset."

"I'm not." Now even her voice sounded too bright. "I'm just not as good at this sort of thing as you are."

"What sort of thing?"

"Flirting. You've probably kissed hundreds of women."

What in the world? When she reached for another paper clip, he leaned forward and placed his hand over hers.

"Just for the record, I haven't kissed hundreds of women." He knew he might be digging his own grave, but he had to take a stand. "And I kissed you because I wanted to."

Casey finally met his gaze, and he felt his equilibrium rock. Of all the lame things to do. Why'd he have to admit something like that? He tried to backpedal, struggling to think what to say. He could hardly admit that she'd been kneeling there, looking incredibly sexy, and then the next thing he'd known, he had her in his arms and was kissing her. He had no choice. He had to finish this discussion. There was too much at stake. His job. His sanity.

"Casey, I think we both agree the kiss was more intense than we expected," he said slowly, trying to gauge her reaction. "But I think we also agree we shouldn't get involved."

"We're not involved. It was just one kiss."

Michael knew he should feel relief at her agreement, but it had been one heck of a kiss. Wait a second. Which side was he on? Annoyed at himself, he pushed on. "I think we need to agree to avoid kissing each other in the future. I personally think it's too dangerous, and we both have other things to concentrate on. So we need to be in complete agreement."

Casey frowned. "That sounds official. Do you want me to sign a contract promising not to kiss you?"

So she wasn't as cool as she pretended. He ran an unsteady hand through his hair. This was turning out to be incredibly difficult.

"Very funny. No. I just don't want us to get distracted from what's important. We need to work on the fundraiser."

She had to know he was right. Deep down, she absolutely had to know he was right. They both had plans. Goals. They couldn't give up now.

His idea made perfect sense.

Finally, she nodded. "Fine. No more kissing."

"Great. No more kissing." The words sounded hollow, and he realized he felt just as empty. What was wrong with him? He was getting what he wanted. He should be dancing on her desk.

"Do we need to shake hands on this deal?" Casey asked.

Michael stood, knowing his best bet was to accept the agreement and leave. "I don't think it's a good idea for us to touch right now."

"Yes. You're probably right."

She picked up another clip, and Michael bit back a groan. Working here was going to be a nightmare.

"I guess we can try to be friends," she said, then she yanked on the clip, distorting it. Destroying it.

Michael made a strangled sound. "I guess that's the option we have."

"Yes. I guess so."

Friends.

Okay, so maybe it wasn't perfect, but it was a lot better than getting involved. And even though he knew Casey would make an amazing lover, he was also certain she'd make a great friend.

And hey, couldn't a guy always use another friend?

❧ 8 ❧

"**S**o, how's it going at the senior center?" Nathan asked as he entered Michael's office the next morning.

Not bad for a bona fide, full-fledged, all-out disaster.

Michael pushed the thought away. "Fine." Which was a huge lie. Yesterday he'd told Casey they should just be friends. And the day had turned out to be one of the longest of his life. Friends were guys you played football with.

They weren't gorgeous, auburn-haired women with sexy eyes who watched your every move. They weren't daydreams that turned around and haunted your nights as well. And they certainly didn't drive you to distraction.

"Really?" Nathan asked.

"Yeah. It's great." He wasn't about to tell Nathan

the truth—that he was incredibly attracted to the center's director.

Nathan chuckled and dropped into one of the chairs in front of Michael's desk. "I think you're full of it. Now tell me the truth."

Michael avoided making eye contact with his boss. "The operation's a lot bigger than I expected, but the director does an excellent job."

"And what have you been doing?"

You mean, besides coming on to the director? Michael shifted in his chair and met Nathan's inquisitive gaze dead-on. "Helping."

Nathan laughed again. "Could you be a little more specific?"

"Why don't you drop by the center and see for yourself?"

A twinkle settled in Nathan's eyes. "Great idea. I think I'll do just that." He considered Michael, then he said, "You still think the time there is hurting the company?"

"Yes. You know as well as I do that this merger is really important," Michael said.

Nathan leaned forward in his chair. "So what do you suggest we do? Back out of our commitment to the community?"

Now that was a good question. Thoughts of Casey and the seniors filtered through Michael's mind. He was torn. Yes, he wanted out of the assignment. Boy, did he ever, especially since he'd kissed

Casey. He'd like nothing better than to spend twelve uncomplicated hours a day at the office.

Aw, but he couldn't just walk away. Maybe it was his past, his father. Or maybe it was the seniors themselves...or Casey. Hell, maybe it was all of that rolled up into one big muddled mess.

"They do need money," Michael said slowly. "So they're making plans to hold a fundraiser at the end of the month."

"What for?"

"Renovations on a new facility."

Nathan nodded. "So help them raise the money."

"I'm going to, but there isn't much time."

With a chuckle, Nathan said, "They need a major miracle—just up your alley. Tell you what, you help with the fundraiser, pull it off, and you're off the hook."

Nathan's pronouncement caught Michael like a swift uppercut to the jaw. "Off the hook?"

"Yep. No more volunteering. You can spend the rest of your days glued to your desk without interruption, if that's what you want." Nathan stood and headed toward the door. "There you go, Michael. You'll be a free man in a matter of weeks."

With that verbal wave of his magic wand, the other man walked out of Michael's office.

A free man. Great. Terrific. Just what he wanted. He ought to be one happy guy.

So why wasn't he?

"Dammit," Michael muttered, slamming shut the

middle drawer on his desk. He was going to be happy about this if it killed him. He'd help with the fundraiser, and when it was over, he'd wish the seniors and Casey well. He might drop by from time to time on his way to a meeting just to say hi. But that would be the extent of it. After the fundraiser ended, he was out of there quicker than a sinner leaving Sunday service.

Casey always knew the moment Michael entered the center, and this afternoon was no exception. The seniors seemed to liven, the volume in the main room increased, and Casey was filled with...expectation.

She glanced out the door of her office and saw him walk across the room, joking and smiling at several of the people. Her heart had developed a funny, flippy rhythm that she'd come to associate with Michael.

She wanted to think of him as simply a friend. A volunteer who would provide invaluable help with the fundraiser, which was good since he'd proven to be a disaster at helping with repairs around the place.

Now if she could only forget the kiss they'd shared. But it lingered in her mind, taunting her senses. And darn it, she wanted to kiss him again. She longed for the same feeling of oneness she'd experienced briefly in his arms.

Michael appealed to her on a lot of levels, not the

least of which was the way he'd fit into the center. She glanced out the door again and saw him sitting at his now usual spot at the men's table with a few of the guys.

Casey had observed the same scene several times over the past few days. She had no idea what the group talked about, but yesterday, Al Terford brought her a handful of money for the swear jar. He muttered an apology, gave her a shy smile, then left.

She'd give the group a few minutes before she gathered them to discuss the fundraiser. Time was running out. Just yesterday, she'd gotten two phone calls from city council members who wanted to know if she could raise the money.

Crossing her fingers, she'd assured them the fundraiser would be a success. Thankfully, neither had pressed her for details, which was either a sign of their supreme confidence in her success or their absolute belief she was going to fall flat on her face. Either way, she owed it to the seniors to find a solution to this problem.

Unfortunately, her mind had turned to a big puddle of mush. Every time she sat down, determined to map out a plan, she'd ended up thinking about Michael. Repeatedly, she reminded herself how friendship offered them a perfect solution.

As friends, they could work beside each other day after day without worrying about emotions getting in the way.

But she knew the plan was worth zip. She couldn't

be friends with this man. He made her stomach swarm with butterflies, her palms sweat, and her breathing get shallow and rapid. She either was developing some really serious illness or an equally bad case of lust. More and more, she got the feeling that friendship just wasn't going to work.

Which left her with...what?

One heck of a problem. She needed to get her priorities straight. Okay, so he was handsome. And he could kiss. But she had to get over this infatuation she felt for him. She had to, so the only solution was to keep busy with the fundraiser. Then she'd have no time to think about Michael Parker. That should do the trick.

At least she sure hoped so.

❦

"So if we just got a band that could play the right sort of music, then I'm sure we could make lots of money," Al said.

"Let it go. You brought that up yesterday, and I told you, we can't get a band if we don't have any money to hire one." Tommy leaned forward and added a swirl of red paint to the ceramic bowl he was painting.

"Yeah, well, it's a good idea anyway." Al turned to Michael. "Don't you think so?"

Michael looked from Al to Tommy and then back again. These two men might be the best of friends, but they fought like old enemies. And Michael liked them both. A lot.

Michael shrugged. "I don't know. Outline your plan."

Al slapped the table, causing Tommy to jump. "Michael, I knew you were a smart man."

"Dang it, Al, you made me ruin my art," Tommy muttered. Frowning, he turned his bowl around, studying the damage.

Since his painting was—put nicely—abstract, Michael wasn't sure how Tommy could tell any harm had been done. But he decided to snuff out the brewing confrontation before Tommy launched into a verbal attack. Michael repeated, "Tell me the plan."

Al leaned back in his chair, and Michael braced himself for pontification. He wasn't disappointed. Before reaching the main point, Al waxed on about life in general for almost ten minutes. Michael was about to say something when Tommy burst out with, "Al, we're old men. Get to the point before Michael has to bury one of us."

With a snort, Al shifted in his chair to face Michael. "Anyway, as I was trying to say before I was interrupted, we should have a Big Band Night. You know, get a snazzy group in, serve a fancy dinner like they used to at the great New York clubs in the late forties, and have dancing. All the town muck-a-mucks will want to come." With a grin, he added, "Great idea, right?"

Michael had to admit, the idea had possibilities. "What did Casey say when you told her?"

"I haven't told her yet. Tommy thought it was a crazy idea since we'd need some money to secure the band and someone to guarantee expenses if we don't raise enough money. I think the city could back us."

"You know they won't," Tommy said, setting his bowl gingerly on the table.

"Like you know anything. You're just jealous 'cause I thought of it."

"Barrett Software could underwrite it," Michael said, startling himself as much as he did both men. They stopped arguing and stared at him.

"You think so?" Al asked.

The more Michael thought about it, the more he liked the idea. "Where would you hold this fundraiser?" he asked.

"I don't know. We can't hold it here. The place is falling apart," Al said.

"I think we could use the cafeteria at Barrett Software. It's huge." Michael shrugged. "I'm sure my boss would go along with it."

"You really think he'd agree?"

At the question, the three men turned. Casey stood behind them. She smiled somewhat self-consciously, her gaze skittering off Michael and landing on the two men. "Let me gather the group, and you can tell us your plan."

When everyone was assembled, Al recapped his plan, ignoring the occasional critiquing from Tommy.

When he finished, Elmira said, "It sounds wonderful."

Al beamed. "I knew you'd like it, Elmira."

"I always said it was an idea with merit," Tommy piped in.

Michael bit back a smile. The two men reminded him of high school rivals. To her credit, Elmira rewarded both of them with an equally bright smile.

"So, do we all agree with Al's idea?" Casey asked.

The group made it clear they more than agreed. "It's going to be a lot of work," Casey pointed out. "And Michael will need to make sure we can hold it at Barrett Software."

"We can do it," Tommy said. "We've got almost three weeks."

Casey laughed, the sweet sound pulling at Michael. He glanced at her and found her watching him. Their gazes met for a long moment, then she looked away. The look she had given him shot his pulse through the roof. He blinked and returned his attention to the group. What had they been talking about?

Oh, yeah. The fundraiser. Now they were in his element. He knew how to put an idea into action, how to give a plan life. For the first time since Casey had told him about the fundraiser, he started to think it might actually happen.

And after that, he'd be gone. He ignored the unexpected sadness that thought brought. All that mattered right now was that the seniors got their money.

Casey glanced briefly at Michael. At some point, he'd taken off his jacket. As he listened to the conversation, he rolled up the sleeves on his white shirt. He picked up a pen off the table and grabbed a couple of sheets of paper.

"So, Casey, where do you want to start?"

She had expected him to hand her the paper and pen like she was his assistant. Instead, he clearly intended on letting her lead the conversation. It drove her nuts when Michael was considerate. How was she supposed to resist him then?

Casey tried to focus on the conversation swirling around them. When Al and Tommy burst into another vocal discussion, she used the distraction to lean slightly toward Michael.

"Thank you for taking notes," she said softly.

Michael shrugged. "Just trying to be a helpful volunteer. But I'll warn you, I'm sure I'll be an opinionated pain-in-the-butt before this is over."

She should be so lucky. If he annoyed her, then maybe she'd stop thinking about how appealing he was. "I'm sure I'll have my fair share of opinions, too."

"Hey, you two, what do you think about Elmira's idea?"

With effort, Casey pulled her gaze away from Michael and forced herself to focus on the group. "I'm sorry, I missed the suggestion."

Elmira moved forward. "I offered a little something extra to the evening. My late husband had a car, a 1970 Dodge Charger, which he just adored. Since his passing, I haven't had the heart to sell it, but I don't want to keep it in storage forever. No one in my family wants it. Do you think..." She waved one manicured hand. "Do you think people might bid for a car?"

"Elmira, we can't let you do that," Casey said, determined not to let the older woman part with something so valuable. "I'm sure your husband's car is worth a lot of money."

"Not really, and I want to donate it," Elmira said. "It's just sitting in the storage shed, costing me money. I've always thought of that car as, well, as almost magical. It's what finally made me fall in love with my husband. A car that special shouldn't be hidden away."

To her amazement, Casey realized from the approving gazes she was receiving that the group was siding with Elmira.

"What? We can't let her make a sacrifice like that," Casey repeated.

"But I want to." Elmira turned toward Michael. "Do you like my idea?"

"I think it's a great idea," Michael said. "But I

have to agree with Casey. We can't let you make that sacrifice."

A sudden warmth crept through Casey, and she struggled to suppress it. But when Michael leaned forward and took Elmira's hands in his, her breath caught in her throat. He looked at the elderly woman with respect and kindness, and Casey couldn't believe she'd ever thought Michael was cold.

Well, yippee and let the cows come home. Working with the seniors was obviously having a positive effect on him.

"Your husband would want you to use that car to help provide for your needs," Michael said to Elmira. "He would—"

"No offense, dear, but he would want me to do what I wanted to do," Elmira said firmly. "And I want to donate it."

Michael turned to Casey. "Looks like the lady has her mind made up."

Casey had to try one more time. "Are you certain about this?"

"Yes. Absolutely." Elmira added with a small smile, "Unless one of you two wants the car. Who knows? That car could put a little magic in your love lives."

Casey refused to look at Michael. "Um, no, thanks."

"I have an idea," Michael said. "We could find out what this car is worth. Then after the auction, we'll pay that amount to Elmira and use any extra cash for the center. Add that money to what the dance brings in, and we...you should be set."

The seniors enthusiastically agreed with his plan.

"That's a great idea," Dottie said. "I knew you were a smart boy." She patted Michael's cheek, then looked at Casey. "And cute, too."

With amazement, Casey watched a tinge of color highlight Michael's face. He was embarrassed. When the seniors continued to fuss over him, she decided to take pity on him.

"Okay, so now that we've settled the car, let's get to work." Casey shot a smile at Michael.

After a second, he smiled back—a sweet, sexy smile that sent Casey's nerves into hyperdrive. Focus. All she needed to do was focus. Then she'd be all set. Yep. All set.

✺ 9 ✺

Michael glanced at Casey as they tugged the cover off Elmira's car. It had been four days since the seniors had come up with the idea for Big Band Night, and Casey was just now able to break free long enough to come see the car.

But coming to the small storage shed together was probably a bad idea. Over the last couple of days, he'd found it increasingly difficult to treat this woman simply as a friend. Now, in the warm, close confines of the storage area, his libido was straying in dangerous directions.

Forcing himself to keep his mind on the task at hand, he helped Casey finish removing the cover. He'd found that the more days he spent at the center, the more he shared Casey's goal. Now, he too wanted Big Band Night to succeed. But not for him. Not even for Casey. He wanted it for the seniors who deserved a center that wasn't falling down around them.

"Wow!" was all he could think to say once he saw the big black car. He'd never been a car nut, but this one might just change his mind. What had Elmira said? The car had made her fall for her husband. He shot a glance at the wide back seat and bit back a chuckle. He could only hope that wasn't what she'd meant.

"This is such a cool car," Casey said. "I can see why Elmira and her husband loved it."

Michael glanced at her, and despite his good intentions, he felt his pulse rate kick up. Tonight she wore her usual outfit—jeans and a T-shirt. Her clothes were perfectly respectable, but somehow, they did a little voodoo dance on his brain. The jeans were just a little snug; the T-shirt molded her curves with loving care. He wouldn't mind getting her into the back seat of that car and seeing what sort of magic they could conjure up.

He blinked. Man, he needed a cold shower—make that a dip in an ice bucket—and right now.

Casey grinned at him over the hood. "Do you think Elmira's right? Do you think this car could be magic?"

Michael pulled his thoughts away from his own little bag of tricks and focused on her question. "Didn't Steven King write a story about a possessed car? Seems to me that didn't work out so well."

Her soft laughter ran across his skin like a warm

breeze, further fanning the flames he'd been trying to douse. "Oh, come on, you have to have a little fantasy in your life."

Oh, he was doing a bang-up job in the fantasy department at the moment. He could see himself tugging her T-shirt free from those tempting jeans. He'd run his hands up her torso, then slowly, with agonizing care, he'd run just the tip of his finger across her—

"Michael? Are you okay? You look kind of funny."

Before he could stop it, a groaning sort of sound escaped his lips. With effort, he switched his hormones off and jump-started his brain. What had she said?

He looked funny. Funny. Yeah, he'd probably looked like a cartoon character with his tongue dragging on the ground and his eyes bugging out of his head. He scrubbed his hand across his face, shaking off the fantasy he'd woven around this woman.

"I'm fine," he managed in a strained voice. "Just fine." Except he wasn't. He was losing his mind in slow degrees to a sexy little siren of a director. Even his dreams were no longer sacred. She'd finagled her way into them in such enticing detail that he often woke up aching for her.

Up until now, he'd never believed a man could die from lust, but he seemed to be giving it one heck of a shot. Worse yet, she wasn't even his type, and although pretty, Casey certainly didn't possess the flawless looks of a model.

Rather, her beauty grew from her personality, fueled by her kindness and humor. Her warmth drew him to her, enticed him into her circle of caring. Just looking at her made desire burn within him, licking at his soul.

He needed to do something about his feelings. The question was—what? A smart man would stop this disaster before it reached titanic proportions. A smart man would back away from this woman—and fast. Well, he might have been a smart man once, but he sure didn't seem to be one anymore.

He took a step forward, toward Casey. That wasn't so difficult. Then he took another. And another. Until he stood directly in front of her.

A tiny frown crossed her brow as she gazed up at him. She must have seen the hunger in his face. "Michael," she said slowly, "I thought we agreed to just be friends."

He trailed his fingers down the side of her face. Her skin was so soft. "I've changed my mind."

"Yep, me too," she said. "I seem to have forgotten my good intentions. We should be ashamed of ourselves."

"Ah, hell, we should be proud of ourselves for lasting this long," he said.

"True," she said. "And you owe me a dollar." Tipping her head, she gave him a flirty smile. "I think the magic of this car is getting to you, hotshot."

Michael backed her up against the car, pressing his body full against hers. "Lady, you have no idea."

When his lips met hers, he didn't even pretend to be a gentleman. He was hungry for her, and he let her know it. It was quickly obvious she shared his hunger. She wrapped around him like a vine, meeting his passion with her own.

It was crazy. It was wild. They were acting like two teenagers in heavy-duty lust. Hands wandered. Lips lingered. The only sound in the tiny storage area was the two of them breathing deeply and murmuring words of pleasure and encouragement.

By tiny degrees, sanity started to seep into the corners of his mind. What in the great blue beyond was he doing? Okay, well, he knew what he was doing, but why? This woman was seriously dangerous to every single plan and goal he'd worked toward for years.

Yeow.

But he figured reason and logic could just wait a couple more minutes. If he was going to do something so beyond stupid that it fell straight into the asinine pit—well, what could an extra few moments hurt?

Especially when she pressed to him harder, and at this particular moment, he couldn't seem to get enough blood to his brain to form a sentence. All he knew was he wanted Casey. Wanted her with a driving need he couldn't seem to contain.

He slid his hands down to her hips and pulled her closer. Rather than being offended, Casey shifted even closer, her body pressed tightly to his.

Oh, yeah. Looked like reason and logic were doomed. Flat-out doomed.

❦

When breathing became almost impossible, Casey tore her lips free from Michael's. For one really long second, she just stared at him. Then reality flooded over her like a bucket of cold water.

She'd gone and done it again. She'd kissed Michael without making the slightest protest. Unless, of course, you considered kissing him back a protest. Sheesh. Where was her mind? Better yet, where were her self-preservation instincts?

"That was a surprise." Casey slipped away from his arms and put as much distance as possible between them.

"It's getting to be more of a habit than a surprise," Michael said.

His rueful tone brought a reluctant smile to Casey's lips. It was a really dangerous habit.

Glancing at her watch, Casey realized she had absolutely no place to be for a couple of hours, so she said, "I'm late for a meeting. Mind driving me back to the center?"

At first, Michael looked like he might object. Finally, with a shrug, he said, "Sure. No problem. We can come back later and start cleaning up the car."

"The car. Right. We'll come back later." Not if she could help it. She'd come back later on her own and clean the car. No way was she coming back here with Michael.

Silently, they left the storage shed and climbed into Michael's Mercedes. Thankfully, once they were driving, Michael turned on the radio, and it covered up the complete lack of conversation between them.

It also gave Casey a chance to gather what little of her wits seemed to be left. She simply couldn't keep kissing Michael. The man lived and breathed his job, so kissing him was playing Russian roulette. Sooner or later it would blow up in her face.

By the time they reached the center, the tension level in the car was sky-high. After parking, Michael turned to face her. When his gaze dropped to her lips, Casey flashed him a warning look.

"This thing between us keeps getting out of control. We need a strict hands-off policy," she said, refusing to dwell on how cute he looked at the moment, with his hair slightly mussed. Okay, so he was cute. Oh, all right, he was sexy as sin. But he was a workaholic, and at times, well, a real pain in the butt. That was what she needed to focus on, not how cute he was.

Even if he was.

"I guess you're right. No more kissing," he said. When she moved to open her door, he placed a restraining hand on her arm. At her questioning look, he said, "But just so you know—I didn't want to stop back there in the storage shed. I couldn't help wishing things would get even more out of control."

LORI WILDE & LIZ ALVIN

Great. That helped a lot.

"Think of something else to wish for," she advised him. Then she slipped out of his car and out of his reach.

For the next two days, Michael avoided Casey and refused to feel guilty about it. He was only doing what a sane man would do. After all, a sane man didn't drop an electrical appliance in his bathtub. And a sane man didn't hang around Casey Richards.

Not unless he wanted to find himself in deep trouble. Because Casey was soft, sweet, and sexy, three deadly traits in a woman. She made him think things best not thought and feel things best not felt.

Emotions made him uncomfortable. They made him antsy. The feelings Casey made dance around inside him were completely new to him. He hadn't grown up with kindness and frankly didn't know how to handle it.

So he'd done the smart thing—he'd avoided her. Not that Casey had exactly sought him out either. Even when he'd hired a handyman to come in and fix the hole in the wall he'd made, she'd just said thanks to him as she walked by on her way to her office this morning. Things would probably work out okay if he just kept his distance from her.

Yeah. Distance. That should solve the problem.

116

"You think Casey needs some help with the decorations?" Al asked.

Michael glanced up from his cards. They were playing a game called Wild Spud. As far as Michael could tell, there were no rules except those that Al or Tommy made up as they went along. At the moment, he had a six, two tens, and two jacks.

All he knew about Wild Spud was that whatever was in his hand was bad and whatever cards Al and Tommy held were good.

"I thought Elmira and Dottie were helping with the decorations." Michael threw down the two jacks, figuring if he was going to lose, he wanted to feel like he deserved to lose.

"They are. But there's not much money in the budget." Tommy picked up the discarded jacks and put them in his hand. Michael wanted to point out that Tommy now had seven cards but decided what the hell. Tommy would simply make up a new rule that allowed the dealer to have more cards than anyone else.

"Barrett Software can help with the decorations." Michael watched in bemusement as Al reached over and took two cards from Tommy's hand, gave him one, then placed the other card in his own hand. Amazingly, Tommy made no comment. What kind of card game was this? Even Go Fish made more sense.

With a grin at Al, Tommy said, "Lookee here, I've got a Wild Spud." He spread his cards out on the table. He had a four, a five, an eight, one jack, and a queen. As far as Michael could tell, the man had zilch.

"Darn your hide." Al tossed his cards on the table. "You're the luckiest Wild Spud player I've ever met." Glancing at Michael, he added, "You should go tell Casey about the decorations."

"Maybe he's scared to talk to Casey." Tommy grinned at Michael. "We couldn't help noticing how you've avoided her ever since the two of you went over to look at Elmira's car. That car didn't work a little magic on you, did it, son?"

Tommy and Al laughed as Michael shook his head. "No, I'm not afraid of her, and no, it didn't work any magic," Michael said, knowing he'd now painted himself into a corner and had to go talk to Casey whether he wanted to or not. "I've been busy the last couple of days. That's the only reason I haven't spoken to her."

Al nudged Tommy. "He's been busy learning to play Wild Spud."

Tommy chuckled. "Yeah. Except he stinks at it."

"How can you tell?" Al asked with a grin. When both men laughed again, suspicion crept up Michael's back like a big bug. "There is no game called Wild Spud, is there? You two were yanking my chain."

"Just having a little fun, Mike. Nothing personal," Al said. "We thought it might do you good to relax a little. We're your friends. Both Tommy and I know men who died way too young by working too hard and being too serious. You're a good man, but you need to pop a few buttons."

Michael laid his cards on the table and looked at the two men. He'd never had anyone care about him before. Not really. It felt nice knowing Al and Tommy considered themselves his friends. He smiled at them and rose to his feet. "Okay, you got me with Wild Spud. And I'll think about the button-popping thing."

"Really?"

He shot a quick glance at Casey's office. "But I'm not afraid of Casey."

Tommy grinned. "Sure you're not, Mike. 'Course not."

Michael groaned as he headed across the room to Casey's office. Behind him, he could hear soft chuckling coming from Tommy and Al. But they were wrong. He wasn't afraid of Casey. No, the lady stirred up all sorts of emotions inside him, but fear wasn't one of them.

In a strange sort of way, he wished it were.

With a flourish, Casey crossed out the final item on her to-do list. She'd finished putting together the proposal for the city council meeting this afternoon and had even remembered to double-check on the cake for Elmira's birthday celebration.

Was she good or what?

Glancing out her open door, she looked over to where Michael was playing cards with Al and Tommy. When she saw him stand and head her way, the now familiar flitter-flutter started in her stomach.

"You're like a sixteen-year-old schoolgirl," she muttered, more than a little annoyed at herself.

"Got a minute?" Michael asked from the doorway to her office. He had an uncertain smile on his face.

Casey wiped her suddenly damp hands on her skirt. Sheesh. What a nutcase she was turning into. She picked up her notes for the presentation, needing something to keep her hands busy. "Sure."

Michael glanced over his shoulder, then entered her office and shut the door behind him. Suddenly they were surrounded by privacy. Being alone with Michael made her as jumpy as a canary at a cat convention.

"First, I want you to know I think you've done a terrific job with this fundraiser. Really amazing," Michael said, walking over to her desk.

"Everyone's done it together." Casey fiddled with the pencils on her desk, avoiding eye contact with him. "I'm just part of the team."

"Most of the work has been yours."

At his gentle words, she made the mistake of looking at him. Aw, drat. His blue eyes held hers with an intense, sexy gaze. She needed to get him out of here. Proximity to Michael was hazardous to her health. Around him, her good sense evaporated.

"Um, thanks." She pulled her gaze away from his

handsome face and restacked the papers for her presentation to the city council.

"You know, Barrett Software has a lot of decorations we can use for the party. That should save us some money," Michael said.

"Great. Thanks for the offer." She half held her breath, hoping he'd now leave.

"No problem."

He gave her that lopsided grin she'd come to know so well, and her heartbeat took off at a run. Desperately wanting a distraction, she tugged on the side drawer of her desk, finally giving it a swift yank to force it open.

"Well, thanks again. Now, if you'll excuse me, I need to find a folder for this presentation. I want it to look nice." Knowing she was prattling, she ducked her head and rummaged through the drawer contents. When no folder floated to the top, she finally started unpacking the drawer. At the very bottom, she found a blue folder.

"Was that all you needed to tell me?" she asked, but when she glanced up at Michael, he wasn't paying attention to her. Instead, he stood looking at the top of her desk.

"What's this?" His hand snaked out, and he grabbed something from under a stack of papers. The second Casey saw the bright-orange cover, she prayed for the floor to split open and swallow her up. Of all the dumb moves.

Ignoring the heat she felt rising on her face, Casey

reached for the book. But with a smooth motion, Michael moved it out of her grasp. He scanned the back cover, then flipped through the pages, a smile tugging at his lips.

He glanced at her. His eyes sparkled with humor and more. The humor she could take. The more left her scared breathless.

A double-dare expression settled on his face, and Casey knew she was in trouble. Why hadn't she insisted Elmira take the book back? Better yet, why hadn't she burned that stupid book? Elmira's grand-daughter didn't need it any more than she did.

"Is this your book, Casey?" His deep voice rippled over her like warm fudge topping.

Good Lord.

"No. It's Elmira's."

He cocked one dark brow. "Really? Elmira's inter-ested in seducing men?"

"No. She loaned it to me because..."

She snatched at the book again, and again Michael held it out of her range. "This is so childish. Just give me the book. It isn't mine, and I intend on giving it back to Elmira."

Michael scanned the book again. "I don't think you should. Seems to me this book contains some interesting ideas." He chuckled. "For instance, Number 72 looks like fun."

He turned the book toward her, keeping it far enough away that she couldn't grab it. Casey frowned at him, but he just laughed again. Then despite herself, she glanced at the book. Number 72 deepened the blush on her face.

"Is that possible?" she asked without meaning to.

Michael turned the book and studied the picture again. For a second, he said nothing, then he gave her a heated look. "I don't know. We could find out."

The thought of being in such an intimate position with Michael made her blood rush like floodwaters. Memories of their kiss a few nights ago flashed through her brain. Funny how she could be so determined to avoid involvement with Michael when he wasn't around, but the second he came near her, all her good intentions disappeared. Still, she made a feeble attempt. "I'm pretty sure we've agreed to just be friends."

The softly spoken words didn't seem to convince him. Rather, Michael moved forward, placing the book on her desk. "Are we? Are you sure?" he muttered, dipping his head.

"Friends don't keep kissing each other," she pointed out, stopping him with a restraining hand on his chest. He felt warm and oh-so-tempting. Reflectively, she contracted her fingers. He sucked in an audible breath.

Michael's gaze never wavered from her own. "I've given this a lot of thought, and I no longer want to be your friend."

10

He had the willpower of a sinner. He'd come into this office determined to tell Casey about the decorations, wish her well this afternoon at the city council meeting, and then make a hasty retreat.

But he'd forgotten everything except his name the second he'd seen that book. Maybe even before he'd seen the book. Around Casey, he had a hard time thinking clearly.

Was that pathetic or what?

At this particular moment, he wasn't thinking at all. He brushed his lips against hers lightly, waiting for her to pull back. Waiting for one of them to have enough sense to stop this nonsense. But she didn't move away. Instead, she came closer, close enough to fit snugly against him. Her hands ran over his shoulders and around his neck.

Danger signals flashed in his brain. He needed to

exercise some basic self-control. Simple as that. The only problem was he seemed sorely lacking in the precious commodity of control.

So when she moaned, he tipped his head and deepened the kiss. She met him with an eagerness that filled him with desire. Need curled through him, wrapping around his heart, his lungs. But even as he explored her mouth, he felt something different in the embrace.

Beneath his desire lay a tenderness he'd never experienced before. Pretty scary stuff. It unnerved him to admit it, even to himself, but he cared for Casey.

Cared about what she felt.

Thankfully, at the moment, she felt like pressing against him. She felt so good; the lady should be illegal.

He moved one hand from her waist and slid it slowly up her torso. She softly said, "Yes."

Knowing he affected her deepened the sensations. It felt right holding this woman, which was both frightening and exhilarating. He nudged her toward the desk. He wanted to make love to Casey. Here. The hell with their surroundings. With convention. Need had turned him crazy.

But noises from the main room drifted through the fog in his brain. Casey wrenched her mouth free from his and pressed her hands against his chest.

"No, Michael. Not here."

He froze as if he'd been tossed into a snowdrift.

With effort, he struggled to get his body under control and drew in several deep breaths, willing his rushing blood to cool.

"Yeah. You're right." His arms still held her tightly. "Just give me a minute here."

Actually, he probably needed closer to an hour. What was it about Casey that turned him into a man who couldn't control his own actions? This time he didn't have a supposedly magical car to blame. This time, the fault was one hundred percent his. He'd always prided himself on his ability to remain emotionally separate from the women in his life. But now, holding Casey, he knew he was fighting a battle he could easily lose.

That was a scary thought. He dropped his arms from around her and moved back. Getting involved with Casey could really screw things up. She would further distract him from his job, which could derail the career path he'd carefully planned for himself.

"Um, Michael, I—" Casey got no further. A brisk tap barely preceded the opening of the door.

"Hi, there." Nathan Barrett walked in, flashing his usual self-confident smile. With him was another older man.

Michael groaned. He'd forgotten Nathan had said this morning he might drop by today. Naturally, Nathan would pick right now to show up. And knowing Nathan, he wouldn't miss a thing. To be honest, the man could have his eyes shut and still know what had just happened in this room. The atmosphere was ripe with tension. Casey looked flushed and mussed and thoroughly kissed. His own appearance probably mirrored hers.

Well, hell.

No sense avoiding the inevitable. Michael met Nathan's quizzical gaze full-on. "Hey, Nathan. Glad you could make it."

Nathan strolled into the office, looking straight at Michael. Then he turned his gaze toward Casey. A smile as big as a canyon split his face.

"Thanks, Michael. I wanted to see for myself all the great things you're doing here."

A soft noise escaped Casey that sounded something like a smothered giggle. Moving farther away from him, she circled her desk, then she extended her hand to Nathan.

"Hi. I'm Casey Richards, the director of the center."

Nathan pumped her hand like a thirsty man working a well. "I'm absolutely delighted to meet you, Casey. This is my father-in-law, Benjamin Montgomery. He's considering moving to Honey and being part of the center."

Michael had never met Nathan's father-in-law, so he shook his hand. Benjamin Montgomery was tall with snow-white hair. He had a friendly, open smile.

"This is a great place," he said.

Nathan nodded. "When I looked into a charity for Michael, I knew he'd be perfect for this place.

Guess I was right. I understand you're planning a fundraiser."

Michael had to hand it to Casey. She looked calm and collected. Still, he couldn't help thinking Nathan's interruption had saved him from making a big mistake. He'd been this close to losing control with Casey.

"We hope Big Band Night will be a success." Casey's voice sounded just a tiny bit husky, reminding Michael all too well what they'd been doing just moments ago. "I hope you'll be able to attend."

Nathan laughed and winked at Michael. "She's a lot like you. She never misses a chance to make a sell." Turning his attention back to Casey, he said, "I'll be happy to help in any way I can."

Benjamin nodded. "I'll definitely be there. It sounds like fun."

An awkward silence settled on the room, and when Casey picked up a stray paper clip, Michael decided to hustle Nathan and Benjamin out of the office before the innocent clip was tortured.

"Let me give you a tour." Michael stepped forward, ushering the men toward the main room. After saying goodbye to Casey, they headed out. Right before leaving her office, Michael glanced back and met Casey's gaze. When she winked at him, he knew he was standing knee-deep in a big pile of trouble.

Casey had barely overcome the kiss with Michael when she had to rush off to the city council meeting. Now she sat facing the members of the council and the mayor and wished she'd brought reinforcements. What was intended to be a nice, simple meeting had turned into a fiasco.

"Look, all I'm trying to do is preview the fundraiser for you. You've already committed the money needed to buy the house," she said, studying their faces. Two of the members, the ones who had assured her repeatedly that everything was fine, refused to look at her. Something was up.

"We've been rethinking the money allocated for the house," one of the council members said. "There's only a few days left, and we doubt you can raise the rest of the needed money."

Annoyance bubbled up in Casey. Oh, no. They were going to play the chase-their-tails game again. It seemed like every time a new council member was elected, everything had to be completely reexamined. Well, she was downright tired of being examined by these people.

"Of course I can raise the money," Casey said firmly. "I've just shown you our plans. Besides, we have to move. The current building is falling apart and unsafe. And much too small."

"Well, maybe we should talk it over again," another council member said. "It is a lot of money."

Sheesh. Good grief. "What's really going on here?"

she demanded, pinning each council member with a hard stare. "Why are you backpedaling?"

Finally, Drew Charlin said, "We're not. It's just this fundraiser you have planned seems risky. What if it doesn't work?"

She glanced at the council members then back at Drew. "Then I'll find another property, and we'll try again. One way or the other, I am going to find a new location for the center."

"Casey, some of the members are new to the council and don't know that much about the center's condition," Drew said. "Why don't you start back at the beginning?"

Oh, for crying out loud! Talk about returning to square one. With a sigh, she settled in her chair, knowing she was in for an annoyingly long meeting.

"Fine, I'll recap why we need the new center, and what changes we envision to our program," Casey said. "Then I'll walk you through the plans for our fundraiser, Big Band Night."

"Michael, I knew this would be the perfect place for you," Nathan said once their brief tour returned them to the main room. "I can see how much influence you're having."

Michael frowned, unhappy with Nathan's assessment. "I haven't done anything." Well, if you didn't count the hole in the wall. "Casey and the seniors have done all the work for the fundraiser."

Nathan dismissed Michael's words with a wave of his hand. "Nonsense. You got me to agree to holding it at Barrett Software."

Before Michael could comment, Benjamin nodded his head toward the far corner of the main room. "There is something I'm curious about. Tell me about that lovely lady."

Huh? Confused, Michael looked across the room. A group of women sat talking. If memory served him, they were in charge of publicity for the fundraiser.

"Who?"

"The beautiful one in the blue dress."

Elmira. Michael should have known. Both Tommy and Al had already treated him to long dissertations on the charms of Elmira Ross. Dottie claimed all men were besotted with Elmira, even without benefit of her magical car.

But for Benjamin to be interested was truly amazing. He'd just moved here, and he was already thinking about his social life.

"Her name is Elmira Ross," Michael said, not sure he liked being a matchmaker for his boss' father-in-law. "She's a very nice lady."

"Married?"

Michael shifted, really uncomfortable with this conversation. He liked Elmira. He felt like a high school freshman. "Widowed."

"Would you mind introducing me?" Benjamin asked.

Michael glanced at Nathan, who had a broad grin on his face. "Yes, please introduce us."

Even expecting the request, it caught Michael off guard. No doubt about it. The center had a strange effect on men. They arrived as perfectly sane but quickly turned into slobbering piles of mush.

Knowing protest would do him no good, Michael led the way across the room. Benjamin Montgomery had guts; he'd give him that. He was about to flirt with Elmira under the very watchful eyes of Dottie and the rest of the ladies.

The man had solid-gold guts.

After introducing Benjamin to the ladies, Michael stepped back and watched the older man in action. He didn't know Benjamin's history, but it quickly became obvious that he hadn't lost the knack of talking to women. Although polite to all of the women, Benjamin managed to convey to Elmira that she held a special interest for him. He asked her questions and listened to her answers with just the right degree of attentiveness. And when he asked his final, go-for-broke question, even Michael held his breath.

"A date?" Elmira's voice rose a tiny bit. "You want to take me out to dinner?"

"Say yes," Dottie hissed. "Or I'll never speak to you again."

Intrigued, Michael watched the scene before him. He glanced at Nathan, who simply shrugged.

An attractive pink tinge settled on Elmira's cheeks. Michael glanced at Benjamin Montgomery. Beguiled. He was definitely beguiled. Elmira was still a heartbreaker.

"I'd like to, but I'm afraid I'm too old for you," Elmira finally said.

Benjamin moved closer. "No, you're not. Please reconsider."

Good manners told Michael to move away, to give these people privacy. But he just couldn't. Natural curiosity forced him to hold his ground until he knew what happened.

"Oh, dear." Elmira looked at Dottie. Then at Michael. And finally at Benjamin. When she smiled, Michael knew Benjamin had won.

"I'd love to go."

Michael felt like giving the older man a high five. He didn't even know Benjamin, but he did know the people at the center. They had a way of getting to people. Heaven knew, these people got to him.

And Casey got to him, too.

❧

Two hours later, Michael knew something was wrong. Casey should have been back by now. Glancing at his watch, he realized she'd never have time to pick up Elmira's birthday cake. He still had some time before

LORI WILDE & LIZ ALVIN

his meeting at four, so he grabbed his coat and headed off to the bakery.

When he got back and Casey still wasn't there, he realized the council meeting must be going badly. Casey never missed a birthday party, and she wouldn't start now with Elmira's. He looked at his watch again.

Damn, if he didn't hurry, he'd miss his meeting. Maybe he could just leave the cake, and the seniors could hold the party themselves. Casey should be here soon.

"Do you think we should start bringing out the plates?" Dottie asked him.

"Actually, I have a meeting—"

Tommy patted him on the back. "That's okay. We can handle this. You head off to your meeting."

Michael glanced around, uncertain what to do. "It is an important meeting," he said lamely.

"You know, we don't need a babysitter," Dottie said. "We can be left alone."

Stunned, Michael turned to stare at her. "I don't think of myself as a babysitter. I know you don't need me to stay."

Tommy nodded. "That's right. So what's the problem?"

The problem? Michael looked from Tommy to Dottie, then to Elmira. Something tugged at him, pulled on emotions he didn't even know he had. He wanted to sing "Happy Birthday" to Elmira, listen to Dottie tease her about her age, and then also listen to Tommy and Al come to her defense. He wanted to stay and be part of the fun and the warmth. Looking at Elmira, he knew he wanted her to know she was special to him.

"The problem is, I want to stay," he admitted, tossing his jacket on the back of a chair. "Let me make a quick phone call, then I'll rustle up some balloons." He grinned at Elmira. "Can't forget the balloons, now can we?"

She'd done it. Was she hot stuff or what? Casey grinned as she locked her car and headed across the parking lot to the center. There had been several times this afternoon when she'd thought the council would turn her down, but somehow, she'd managed to slam-dunk the presentation.

And now she felt terrific. She could hardly wait to tell the seniors. And Michael.

Shoving open the door to the center, she was all set to share the great news when she noticed the scene before her and stumbled to a stop. Cake. Party plates. Balloons.

Oh, no. She'd forgotten Elmira's birthday party.

"Oh, my God," she whispered. From the look of things, the party was over. Most of the seniors were gone. Only a few remained, and they were picking up. How could she forget something so important? Elmira was like a member of her own family. Casey loved her. Images of her own birthday parties as a child hit her. Her parents, always so wrapped up in their jobs, would arrive just as the party ended. If they arrived at all.

She was a horse's patootie. Glancing around, she saw Michael walk out of her office talking to Elmira. When he noticed her, he smiled and waved her over.

"Elmira, I'm so very sorry," she said when she reached the older woman's side. "The meeting ran late, and I didn't dare leave until they agreed to Big Band Night. Please forgive me."

Elmira patted her arm. "That's okay, dear. No harm done. But if you'll excuse me, I'm in a bit of a hurry."

With a final wave, Elmira walked out. From her distracted attitude, Casey didn't believe for a second that the older woman forgave her. With a mental kick to herself, she turned to Michael. "Thanks for staying."

"No problem. I stayed because I wanted to. So how did everything go this afternoon?"

Casey picked up one of the balloons. "They agreed to our plans. Finally."

"Great." He frowned. "You okay?"

No.

"Sure. Well, I know you need to get back to your office," she said, her voice overly bright even to her own ears. "And I need to work out some last-minute details."

Casey thought he would argue with her, but eventually, he said, "I'll see you tomorrow."

"Tomorrow, yes." Then she walked into her office, quietly shutting the door. How in the world had she forgotten? She hadn't just been late. She'd gotten so caught up in the meeting that she'd completely forgotten about Elmira's birthday party.

Right now, she felt like pond scum. No, it was worse than that—she was so low, she was whatever pond scum despised.

𝕾 I I 𝕾

Michael felt like a fool as he climbed the stairs to Casey's apartment. Only a fool would rush through an important meeting so he could go check on a...a what? What was Casey to him? A friend?

No. She was right. Friends didn't kiss the way they did. No, Casey was a woman who made him feel like he was riding a roller coaster. Dealing with her was both exhilarating and terrifying.

But today, something strange had happened. He'd worried about her. She seemed so unhappy when he'd left her at the center. Worrying about someone was a brand-spanking-new experience for him.

An uncomfortable experience that made it difficult for him to concentrate on his meeting. Was this what people with families felt all the time? That they should be somewhere else? It was like being dragged in two different directions by wild horses—not exactly a sensation he wanted to duplicate on a regular basis.

But, fool or not, he had to make certain Casey was all right. So he'd come to see for himself that she was fine. He tapped lightly on her door and waited, uncertain of what to expect.

When she opened the door and he saw her face, he knew he'd been right. She was upset. Her eyes were red-rimmed. His heart twisted when he realized she'd been crying.

"Mind if I come in?" Michael asked.

Casey stood staring at him as if he'd dropped from the sky. Finally, she moved aside so he could enter.

"What are you doing here?" she asked, shutting and locking the door behind him.

Michael didn't answer right away, wanting to first gauge her mood. So instead, he moved into the living room, noticing how it reflected Casey's personality. Two brightly flowered, overstuffed couches filled the small room.

Flowers tumbled out of an eclectic assortment of vases, giving the room a cozy feel, and books lined several long shelves. Casey had created a warm room, an inviting room. A room just like her.

Michael turned to face Casey. "I came to make sure you're okay. You seemed upset this afternoon."

Casey nibbled on her bottom lip, and Michael sensed she wanted to talk about it. Deciding to make it easier, he said, "You feel bad about missing the party, right?"

Wordlessly, Casey nodded, the gleam in her eyes telling him she wasn't far from tears again. "I can't believe I missed it."

He gently took her hand in his. Warmth tingled through his fingers. He led her over to one of the couches and sat, pulling her down next to him. When she settled deep into the cushions, he turned to face her.

"You had to go to the council meeting. Elmira understands that," he said emphatically. The unhappiness he saw on her face tugged at him. His need to console her was making him damn nervous. He didn't need a metal detector to know he was smack-dab in the middle of an emotional minefield when it came to this woman. She stirred up all sorts of foreign feelings, and to a man like him, a man who made a point of never getting seriously involved, feelings were the bogeyman. Something scary enough to make him turn tail and run.

But right now, he didn't feel like running. He also didn't want to put a name to these new feelings. Hey, just because he cared about Casey didn't mean he'd totally lost his mind. Just maybe misplaced it temporarily.

Casey sighed. "Being at the party was important to me."

Michael shifted closer to her on the sofa. He didn't even try to be coy. He boldly slipped his arm behind her and gathered her to his side. Dipping his head, he said softly, "And why is that?"

He half expected Casey to refuse to explain, or to at least move out of the circle of his arms. But she did neither. If anything, she snuggled deeper against him.

"Birthdays are special to me."

Brushing a stray strand of hair off her forehead, he asked, "Now why is that?"

She looked faintly self-conscious. "It's silly, really."

"Tell me," he prompted, wanting to understand.

"I wanted Elmira to know I care," Casey said.

"She does. She understood. You had to secure the funding for the center." He frowned, sensing there was something more here. "What's really bothering you?"

With a shake of her head, Casey said, "Never mind. I told you it was silly."

"I won't think it's silly," he said, his gaze never leaving her face. "Well, not unless you tell me you've always secretly wanted to be a clown because you admire their wardrobes."

Casey gave him a faint smile, and he felt some of the tightness around his heart ease.

She shot him a brief glance, then blurted, "See, my parents missed almost every birthday party I ever had. They always had the nanny throw them, and they rarely showed up. They only cared about work."

Silently, Michael willed her to go on.

"I know it sounds crazy," she finally added. "But

141

the more parties they missed, the more I wanted them there."

Michael was half-afraid he knew the answer to the question hovering on his lips. Since there was no sense avoiding the inevitable, he bit the bullet and asked, "Why weren't your parents there?"

She gave him a rueful smile. "They were always working. Always too busy to spend any time with me. So they missed birthday parties, holidays, and even Christmas. My father was a true-blue corporate shark. My mother traveled for her job and was rarely home."

Ouch. Michael pushed away memories of how he'd spent Christmas last year at his desk, eating vending-machine cuisine. Hey, he could spend Christmas by himself if he wanted to. He didn't have a family waiting on him.

But in a way, Casey's parents had been as selfish as Michael's old man had been. None of them made a place in their lives for their children.

As he'd come to realize, priorities are important.

This little history lesson sure explained Casey's attitude toward him. She thought that as soon as something important came up at the office, he'd bail on her quicker than a gigolo after the check cleared.

Which, of course, was exactly what he planned on doing after the fundraiser.

He pushed aside that anvil-sized block of guilt and focused instead on Casey. Hoping to put a positive spin on this, he asked, "So your parents were into their jobs?"

"That's all they cared about. All they ever thought about."

"And that still bothers you," he said.

"Not really." At his dubious look, she added, "Only in as much as I don't want that kind of obsession in my life. I don't ever want to be that kind of person. To me, life's about more than the next deadline, the next promotion." She shot him an apologetic look. "No offense."

At any other time, Michael would have complimented her on the swift verbal blow to his chin, but he let it slip by. Sure, in his book, working hard was important, but he wasn't so callous that he couldn't understand how long days at the office would strike a child as not caring.

"Your parents probably worked hard so they could make a good life for their family."

She shook her head. "It was more than that. Both of them felt their job was always their first priority. Their jobs were their whole world, and it didn't seem to matter if they disappointed me. I'm still not sure why they even had a child because neither of them wanted to spend time with me. I vowed when I was young to not be that type of person."

This conversation was hitting a little too close to home for Michael, so he decided to fandango it in a new direction. "Well, I wouldn't worry about Elmira.

She's an adult and knows you wanted to be at the party."

He sensed Casey wanted to believe him but didn't.

"It doesn't matter what your age is," she said. "You can still have your feelings hurt."

There were those scary feelings, raising their evil little heads again. Up until a week or so ago, he'd pretty much been able to steer around those bugaboos. But feelings for Casey had brought him here tonight, and feelings for Casey prompted him to say, "Why don't you call Elmira and talk to her?"

Casey studied him. "Do you really think I should?"

Like he was an expert on the polite thing to do. Still, he said, "Yes." He shifted away and picked up the portable phone from the end table. "Do you know her number?"

Casey nodded. "Elmira and I sometimes talk in the evenings."

Michael stood and moved across the room while Casey made her call. In a couple of minutes, he knew from the happy tone in Casey's voice that Elmira wasn't upset. With a smile on his face, Michael wandered into the kitchen.

And found ducks. A lot of ducks. Flocks of ducks. Ducks on the wallpaper. Ducks on the dishtowels.

Ducks on the oval throw rug on the floor in front of the stove. On one white counter, a large ceramic duck held an assortment of cooking utensils. Then, perched on the side of the sink was another duck with a large blue sponge in its mouth.

Holy...duck.

"You were right," Casey announced from the doorway. "She wasn't upset. She said she knew the meeting was important."

Michael turned toward her, thrilled to see a genuine smile on her face. "Great."

"Actually, she was giddy when I talked to her." Casey leaned against the oak table in the corner of the kitchen. "Apparently, she's getting ready for a date with your boss' father-in-law."

"Oh, yeah, they hit it off while you were at your meeting." He moved toward the door, suddenly uncertain what to say. "I'm glad everything worked out."

"Thanks." She shifted a duck spoon holder around on the table. "Any chance I could convince you to stay for dinner? I'd like to thank you for...tonight." She smiled. "I can't promise anything fancy, so you'd have to settle for potluck."

Of course, a smart man would leave before he got himself in trouble. But then again, a smart man wouldn't have come here in the first place. Hadn't he already decided he was a fool? No sense being a fool with an empty stomach. "Potluck? Exactly what does that mean?"

Casey tossed a duck-covered dishtowel at him, which he caught with one hand. "It means you're lucky you're getting fed at all."

With a grin, Michael placed the towel on the counter. He liked the sparkle in Casey's eyes, the happiness in her smile. There was no sense kidding himself—he wasn't going to be leaving for a while.

"Then I guess I'd better help, just so I can make certain this potluck of yours is safe to eat," he said.

"Trust me, you'll be safe."

Yeah, Michael amended in his mind, but maybe not smart.

"I was wondering if you could help me finish waxing Elmira's car tomorrow," Casey said, stacking the rest of the dishes in the dishwasher. She glanced over at Michael. Dinner had been fun. They'd kept the conversation light and impersonal. "I've moved the car over to the center so we can finish getting it ready."

"Sure. I'll help," Michael said as he wiped the table. "Tommy and Al told me you've been working on it. So what do you think? Is it magic?"

Casey shrugged, suddenly wanting to talk about anything but magical cars that made you fall in love. Truthfully, she didn't believe a word of that nonsense, mostly because she and Michael didn't need to be anywhere near the classic car for their hormones to fly out of control.

"I think Elmira would have fallen for her husband without the car," Casey said, suddenly realizing how cozy she and Michael were in her tiny kitchen.

Michael crossed the room and stopped directly in front of her. He had a teasing gleam in his eyes that was incredibly appealing.

"Aw, come on," he said. "Don't blow an age-old belief right out of the water. Men have been buying fancy cars to impress women for years. Don't tell me that trick doesn't work when I've just bought a brand-new Mercedes."

No fair. Michael was attractive at the worst of times, but when he was teasing with her, he was downright irresistible. Needing to put some distance between them, Casey led the way out of the kitchen and to the living room.

"Okay, I won't totally discount the theory," she said. "But I still don't believe the car is magical. If it were, we could auction it off for a lot more money."

Michael laughed, the deep rumble coursing through Casey. "Your bottom line is showing."

She smiled and sat down on the sofa, tucking her feet under her. "I guess there's a little of my parents in me, after all. Anyway, let's talk about something else. I told you about my family. What was your childhood like?"

Oops. Wrong question. She watched Michael tense.

"You don't have to talk about it if you don't want to," she said quickly. "We can talk about the fundraiser instead."

Michael sat near her on the sofa. "No. It's okay. Let's just say I just didn't have a Norman Rockwell-style upbringing either."

Indecision filled Casey. She wanted to respect his privacy, but she also wanted to know more about him.

"Were you an only child?" she asked.

His blue gaze sought and held hers. Reaching out, he took her hand, winding his fingers through hers. Michael looked at their joined hands.

"You really want to hear this?" At her nod, he sighed. "You may regret asking, but okay. Yes, I'm an only child."

"Where did you grow up?"

"Mostly on an old ranch in West Texas."

"You were a cowboy?"

He immediately said, "Not on our ranch. We only had one horse and not much else. But I did work on neighboring ranches when I was growing up."

"I'm sure your parents——"

"Casey, before this turns into a daytime talk show, let me sum it up for you. My mother left when I was a toddler. My father tried, I guess, but he had a heartfelt aversion to work. Of any kind. So he rarely participated." He glanced at her. "He wasn't really mean to me. Just unaware that I was around."

"Oh. I'm sorry."

He shrugged. "Don't be. My childhood taught me to appreciate hard work and the benefits gained from it. I enjoyed working on the neighboring ranches. They taught me that hard work has rewards."

"Like being able to buy a car that impresses women?" she teased.

Michael smiled. "Maybe. But it's also about having food and a place to live that isn't about to be condemned. It's about feeling your life means something." His blue gaze caught and held her attention. "It's about making a difference."

Boy, did she ever know what he meant. She felt exactly the same way, except she didn't want to make a difference by pulling in a big paycheck. She wanted to bring joy to the people in her life. She struggled to keep her voice steady as she asked, "Where's your father now?"

"Dead. He died the second year I was scrapping my way through college." Michael turned toward her, his large hand cupping her cheek. "Bet you're sorry you asked about my family now."

Blinking, Casey covered his hand with her own and leaned against his palm. He felt warm and secure. And exciting. Very exciting. "To tell you the truth, I'm proud of you."

He stilled. "Proud?"

"Yes." Tenderness for Michael overwhelmed her. How could she have ever thought he was a heartless shark? He'd come here tonight just to make certain she was okay. Not exactly the actions of a man with no heart.

"I'm proud of the man you've become, of the things you overcame," she said. "Look at what you've accomplished."

He started to lean toward her when abruptly he stopped. A groan escaped him seconds before he pulled away from her. "I'd better go."

Drat. She must have said the wrong thing. Casey halted him before he stood. "I didn't mean—"

"You know, I'm sorry, but I can't do this." He leaned back out of her reach. "I shouldn't have told you about my past. I don't want your sympathy."

Sympathy? He thought what she felt for him was sympathy? Casey bit back a laugh and watched as he stood and took two steps away. Then she said, "I don't feel sympathy for you."

He turned and looked at her, his blue eyes darkening dangerously. "You don't?"

She stared at him, her heart in her throat, her palms sweating. Didn't he feel it? The sexual pull between them was so strong she felt it like an undertow. Dragging her toward him. Making rational thought impossible. Even now, looking into his mesmerizing blue eyes, she felt herself falling like Alice down the rabbit hole. She wanted to kiss him, to touch him, to drink her fill of him.

"Oh, Michael, what I feel is desire," she said, her voice a mere whisper in the quiet room.

"Desire," Michael repeated, his gaze never leaving her face. He hadn't expected her to say that. Slowly, he moved back to the couch, and when he stood in front of her, he brushed the back of his fingers across her cheek. She shivered, and he knew he was lost.

"Casey, are you sure?"

She nodded once, and that was all he needed. He gathered her into his arms, finding her mouth with an overwhelming urgency. When she slid her arms around his neck and kissed him deeply. He wanted as much as he could get, needing this woman so much it defied logic.

He'd never experienced such intense emotions. Truthfully, he'd never really experienced any emotions when it came to sex. It had always been about physical needs. But with Casey, it was so much more than just lust. He wanted her body, but he also wanted something more. Something he couldn't name but felt with equal urgency.

With effort, he pulled his lips away from hers. "Are you really sure?" he rasped, not wanting to think about the possibility of her saying no. His heart skipped a beat when she smiled at him.

"Yes, I'm really, really sure." Tipping her head, she asked, "What about you? Are you really, really sure? I don't want you waking up in the morning and claiming I seduced you."

Michael chuckled. "Don't worry about that. I want to be seduced."

She climbed off the couch and took his hand. "In that case, my bedroom is this way."

Michael hadn't left her, Casey realized with a start when she awoke in the middle of the night. Instead, he lay sprawled next to her, his arm tossed across her stomach. Turning her head, she watched him in the moonlight seeping through her thin drapes. Michael asleep was a marvel. Awake, he always seemed busy, doing something, rushing somewhere. Asleep, he looked so peaceful it reminded her just how sweet and tender he could be.

She sighed. Now, why'd she have to go and fall in love with a corporate shark? But she was in love with him. No doubt about it. The feeling washed over her, and she realized she was hopelessly, completely, probably stupidly in love with Michael. Her heart had made its own decision, and there was nothing she could do about it. She could either go looking for trouble or just accept what had happened. Granted, this affair of theirs couldn't go anywhere. After the fundraiser, Michael no doubt would be back to working nonstop. And she would be busy with the modifications on the new center.

Still, there was now, this night, and the other nights between now and the fundraiser in a few days. Was there any reason why she couldn't grab the happiness she had within her grasp without worrying about tomorrow? Sooner or later, she knew this thing between them would end, but why did it have to be sooner?

The arm across her tightened. "You're thinking so

hard, I can hear you," Michael drawled, his voice sleepy. "Are you making plans for the new center?"

Casey smiled. "No. I was thinking about you."

With a chuckle, he rolled over to face her. Propping his head on one hand, he said, "I hope you're thinking good things."

"Yes."

"No regrets?" She could hear the tension in his voice.

"No." Glancing behind him, Casey noticed a faint glimmer in the moonlight. Smiling, she decided she wanted whatever time she could have with him. She needed this. These precious days would keep her going long after she and Michael had gone their separate ways.

"I was just thinking about how wonderful you are," she said.

Michael grinned. "Let me demonstrate again just how wonderful I can be."

And then he kissed her.

🌾 12 🌾

Michael sat in his office Thursday afternoon staring out the large window behind his desk. Big Band Night was on Saturday, and he still hadn't told Casey he wouldn't be coming back after that.

You might as well paint a yellow stripe down his back and call him a coward. Because that's what he was. A coward. He'd meant to tell her. He really had. But things between them were so great he didn't want to rock the boat.

Telling Casey he wasn't going to help at the center anymore would more than rock the boat. It would sink it straight to the ocean floor. More than likely, Casey would take his leaving as further proof that he really was an unrelenting workaholic who only cared about his job.

But that wasn't true. He cared about Casey, too, and didn't want their affair to end. Not now. Not when things between them were so spectacular that his life felt perfect for the very first time. It was selfish of him, but he didn't want to stop being with Casey.

Still, he had to be honest with her. After the fundraiser, he couldn't afford to spend any more time away from work. Turning back to his computer, he studied the piles of paper on his desk. He had to be crazy to be thinking about Casey now. His work needed his full attention for the next few weeks, if not months, and yet here he sat, mooning over Casey. He had to face facts—he didn't have time for an affair, especially a hot, wild, all-consuming, amazing affair. Being with Casey was a distraction.

A major, serious distraction that could easily cost him a promotion if he didn't watch himself. He needed one hundred percent of his concentration focused on work. Then he had a real shot at ensuring the merger happened without a hitch. He wanted to do a great job. He wanted to be successful.

And if the merger went off without a hitch, a promotion was definitely in his future. Nathan had mentioned a couple of days ago that the merger would help them expand the company, which would ensure promotions for many people.

Michael knew he couldn't lose his focus now. Not now when everything he'd ever wanted was almost within his grasp. If he continued to see Casey, she'd need to understand about his job.

Which meant there was a pretty good chance

Casey would tell him to buzz off. But still, maybe they could reach a compromise.

They were both intelligent, reasonable people. Maybe, despite the way her parents had treated her, maybe she'd understand if he couldn't be with her very often over the next couple of months, and maybe just as soon as the merger crisis ended, they could be together more.

Michael sighed. It would be easier to convince Casey that he was the Easter Bunny than convince her the merger would be the last crisis dropped in his lap.

There was always a crisis or opportunity at work, and everyone depended on him to do his part. They would depend on him even more if he got promoted.

"Drat," he muttered, then smiled. Casey sure had him trained. He couldn't even curse in the privacy of his own office anymore without wanting to pay someone a dollar.

There had to be a solution to this problem. He didn't want to stop seeing Casey, but he knew she deserved better than a man who was hardly ever with her, a part-time lover who came to see her only when his schedule allowed it.

Which, unfortunately, was all he had to offer. Well, the only fair thing was to let Casey decide. She needed to make up her own mind, and he'd just have to live with the consequences.

He'd also pray she didn't ask him to put his feelings for her into words because he flat out couldn't.

Was what they had love? How would he know? He didn't know what love looked like, how it felt.

And it wasn't as if there was a standardized test you could take to find out for sure. No, figuring out his feelings was going to be a lot more difficult than choosing: A—She has a great laugh. B—She makes me smile. Or C—She really, really turns me on.

Of course, he'd have to choose D—All of the above.

But was that love or just really great lust? He didn't know. All he knew was he wanted to keep seeing her as much as their schedules allowed. So tonight, he'd take her out to a romantic dinner, explain how important she was to him, and then see if there was a compromise they could reach. After that, he'd pray she didn't tell him to take a flying leap.

Because if she did, he didn't know what he'd do.

<hr />

"I'm never going to find something to wear." Casey paced around her bedroom, tossing dress after dress on her bed. Sheesh. There was no reason for her to be nervous. They'd spent the last three nights making love in her bed. Still, she'd been jumpy since Michael had asked her out today when he'd been at the center. He'd seemed so serious that she got the feeling he wanted to talk.

For them, talking could only lead to trouble. Really big trouble. Maybe he'd decided he didn't want to see her anymore. Maybe he'd realized their being together was a huge mistake. Which, of course, it was. They both had things to accomplish in life, and they certainly didn't have time for a relationship.

But she wanted to be with him. Love flowed through her for Michael. How could he not feel the same magic? He had to. If she were a brave woman, she'd ask him how he felt, demand he admit he loved her back. She knew she wouldn't do it, though. In some ways, she was brave. But not brave enough to ask Michael if he loved her.

She finally decided to wear a short black dress. Placing it on her bed, she reached for her perfume and dabbed a drop between her breasts. Before she could slip into the dress, she heard a definite knock on her door. She looked at the clock. It was seven. It was Michael.

Feeling mischievous, she vetoed the dress and put on her robe instead. When she opened the front door, the sight of Michael looking tall and handsome and sexy did nothing to settle her already frazzled nerves. Yep, she wasn't brave at all. But she knew he felt the magic between them, too. She could see it in his heated gaze.

"Hi," he said in that deep voice that made shivers run up her spine. "You look great."

She laughed. "No, you look terrific. I'm in my bathrobe."

He raised one dark brow. "Need some help getting

dressed?" he asked as he moved farther into her apartment, closing the door behind him.

Looking up at him, Casey felt her love for this man lodge in her throat. She couldn't ask him how he felt, but she could show him her feelings.

"Let's stay here," she blurted out.

"Here?" He studied her for a moment, then grinned.

"Yes." Her voice sounded husky, laden with desire. "And talk?"

Casey sucked in a deep breath. "No." With one pull, the knot came undone on her robe. The sides parted. Now seemed like a good time to go for broke, so she shrugged the robe off her shoulders. It dropped to the floor, leaving her standing in only her strapless black bra and panties.

Silence settled on the room, broken only by the ticking of the grandfather clock in the corner of the living room. Casey would have felt incredibly self-conscious if it hadn't been for the way Michael's gaze wandered over her, lingering occasionally on things he apparently found interesting.

The look he gave her when his gaze returned to her face was nothing short of incendiary. Wearing a tiny smile, she took a step forward. Then another. And finally, she took the last step that brought her directly in front of him.

In that moment, standing before Michael and looking up into his handsome face, Casey felt as if she were drowning and going down for the third

159

time. Her love for Michael overwhelmed her. Even if he was the wrong man, she loved him. And the thought of that love filled her with joy.

Michael slid one strong arm around her waist, pulling her flush against his body. He bent his head and found her lips. This time, his kiss didn't start out gentle. Instead, the kiss was about hunger and need. About temptation and fulfillment. Casey wrapped her arms around his neck, meeting his urgency with her own. Then he startled her by lifting her off the ground.

"I'm too heavy," she said, looking deep into his darkened blue eyes. "I don't want you to strain anything."

Michael chuckled as he carried her the few feet to her bedroom without showing the slightest sign of difficulty. "I get the feeling there's a purely selfish motive behind your concern."

As he walked, he never took his gaze off her face. Love spilled through Casey like a waterfall. They hadn't settled anything about their future. She knew that, but she had tonight with him. And maybe tomorrow.

And that would have to be enough.

When Casey awoke the next morning, she pulled on her robe, and padded down the hall.

When she reached the kitchen, Michael gave her

such a sexy look she decided to play it safe and stay on the opposite side of the table while he poured some coffee and put bread in the toaster.

"Why don't you come over here?" he asked when she evaded his grasp.

Casey shook her head. "You said you wanted breakfast. I'm hungry, and when I get near you, we both seem to have trouble keeping track of our hands."

"I don't mind."

She shook her head again. "Because you're a good sport."

He started to say something, but the toast was done. Grabbing a piece, he buttered it and handed it to her. "Here's food. As promised."

Taking the other piece of toast for himself, he ate it slowly.

"Aren't you going to butter that?" she asked, unable to stop staring at him.

"No. I'm in a hurry to finish breakfast."

Casey smiled. "Now why is that?"

"Have you had enough to eat?" he asked rather than answering her question. Slowly, deliberately, he circled the table, a heart-stopping grin forming on his face as he gathered her close.

"Michael," she murmured, burying her face in his shoulder. When she lifted her head, he smiled. "What are we going to do?"

"We're smart people. We can figure this out." He kissed her and gave her a wry smile, his gaze direct and intense. A knot formed in her throat. Something was up. She could tell.

"Casey...you mean a lot to me," he said softly.

Oh, no. That didn't sound good. "Um, me...too."

"I feel whole when I'm with you," he finished, his voice thick and husky.

Okay. That didn't sound as bad. Right now would be a good time to tell him she loved him. But as overwhelming and wonderful as the thought of Michael caring for her was, she sensed there was more to come.

"But?" she prompted.

He looked away, his jaw tight. She held her breath, willing him to say he loved her, that he'd be with her, that he'd put her before his job. But that was asking for the moon.

After an eternity, he glanced back at her. "As soon as the fundraiser is over, I need to go back to work full-time."

Casey turned his words over in her mind. He wasn't going to volunteer anymore, but she really wasn't surprised. She'd expected this. Michael wanted to go back to working fourteen-hour days. To living and breathing his job.

Moving away from him, she carried her plate to the sink. "I understand." And she did. He wanted to spend all his time at work, so this was the end of them.

"No. You don't," Michael said.

Bracing herself, she turned to face him, trying to

force air into lungs that seemed to have forgotten how to breathe. "So what are you saying?"

"I think we should live together."

❦

Man, he hadn't intended on saying that. He hadn't intended on saying anything remotely like that. But that was what Casey did to him. She made him do things completely out of character. But when the words jumped out of his mouth, he realized he meant them. He wanted to live with Casey so he could at least see her every night.

Casey, though, stood staring at him as if he'd been possessed by a demon.

"You're kidding," she said.

He realized she wasn't asking a question but making a statement. "No." He moved forward and took her hands in his. "I guess you know that once I go back to work, I'll have to put in long hours." Before she could say anything, he added, "But you'll have to put in some long days at the new center."

Casey slowly sank into one of the high-backed kitchen chairs. "Michael, I don't—"

He moved to stand directly in front of her. "What bothers you about the idea?"

Casey shrugged. "Everything."

"Such as?" He sat in the chair next to her, forcing himself to stay calm. But it was hard. He wanted her to say yes.

"Have you thought this through?" she asked. He hadn't, but he wasn't about to admit that. Because now that he'd suggested the idea, he was convinced it would work. "I'm certain."

She leaned forward, her scent surrounding him. "I think it's just the sex—"

"This isn't about sex, Casey. This is about..."

Her intense gaze focused on him. "About what?"

What was it about? Love? He didn't know. "It's about caring for each other. I enjoy being with you." His words were tame compared to the emotions surging through him. Casey's expression made it clear she wasn't swayed by what he'd said.

"I don't think it will work," she said quietly.

"What do you feel for me?" he asked.

Wide-eyed, Casey blinked at him. "I'm in love with you," she said, her voice brushing over his skin.

He hadn't expected that. A surge of happiness shot through him. He pulled her into his arms. "Then don't say no. We can make it work."

"Michael, we're so different," she protested. "Your job is everything to you. And I need a man who will be there for me."

He bent to kiss her sweet, sexy lips. "My job's not everything. Sure, I love my job, but I'll make this work, too. I promise you. I'll make this work."

Knowing it wasn't fair, he kissed her before she could argue. As always, she melted against him, and he knew he would keep his promise. He would find a way to make this work.

Resting his forehead against hers, he said, "Just think about it, okay? Please, think about it."

He held his breath until she nodded. Then he knew everything would be all right. Everything would be fine.

❦

Casey finished polishing the hood of the old Charger and stood back to admire her handiwork. Boy, if she could afford it, she'd buy this gorgeous car in a heartbeat.

"Hello, Casey," Elmira said, coming to stand next to her. "You look very happy today."

Casey wasn't sure she'd call herself happy. Sure, the plans for Big Band Night were coming along nicely. And sure, everyone's spirits were high, and Casey was thrilled for the seniors. And sure, it was definitely starting to look like the fundraiser would work.

But was she happy? Tough question. She still didn't know what to do about Michael.

"I'm doing okay," she finally said.

Elmira nodded. "I understand." With a quick pat on Casey's arm, she added, "Hon, men are like shoes. It takes a while to break them in."

Casey laughed. "Shoes?"

Elmira glanced over Casey's shoulder, then gave her a conspiratorial wink. "I think Michael's coming over to help you. I'll go...um, check on my...surfboard.

Have fun."

As Elmira hurried away, Casey heard Michael walk up behind her. Gathering her courage, she turned to face him. Ever since they'd become lovers, they'd pretty much left their personal relationship outside the center. Although judging from Elmira's words, the seniors knew all about them.

"Hi," he said.

"Hi." She wiped her hands on her jeans. "I think the car's about ready for tomorrow night."

He stood back and studied the car. "So I see. Anything I can do to help you?"

Sure. Fall in love with me. Deliberately, she moved away from him. She needed time to think. She'd never really considered living with a man before, for a lot of reasons. The main one being she'd never been in love before.

But she was now, and like Michael, she wanted to spend whatever time they could find together. But was that building a future or just postponing the inevitable? When push came to shove, would he choose business over her? Would she end up bitter about the days and nights she spent alone? Casey couldn't let that happen to her.

"Can I help?" Michael repeated.

She blinked and turned to face him. "Al and Tommy are finishing the final preparations for the auction. Maybe you can help them."

When she started to walk past him, he blocked her way. He placed one hand on her shoulder, the warmth of his touch having its usual effect on her hormones. "Casey, have you thought about what I suggested this morning?"

"Yes."

"And?"

She looked up into his face, love filling her. How could she say no? But how could she say yes? Reluctantly, she said, "I don't think it's a good idea."

"Why not? You said you love me."

She didn't want to make this choice. Not now. "I do love you, but like I said, I think we're too different."

"We can work out any problems," he rasped, moving closer to her. "If we want to."

She looked beyond him. Several of the seniors were milling about, and Al was heading their way. "Do you love me?" she whispered.

Now it was Michael's turn to stare at her. "I care about you—"

She waved one hand. "That's not the same. Do you love me?"

His silence pretty much answered her question. Finally, he said, "I don't think I know how to love."

Not the answer she wanted. The world seemed to lurch beneath her feet, but she couldn't waver.

"Then you have to learn before we can have a future."

"Casey, don't do this. I just need some time to sort through what I'm feeling. All I know is you're too precious to me to lose."

"Can we talk about this later?" she asked, feeling self-conscious having this conversation at the center.

Michael seemed oblivious to the seniors. "Fine. Later. Just tell me one thing; why won't you live with me if you love me?"

Sheesh. He was making this difficult. She would prefer to stand in the middle of a room of super-models with a serious case of bedhead rather than tell Michael the truth, but she couldn't lie to him.

"I won't live with you because I don't trust you to be there when I need you," she said.

❧ 13 ❧

On the drive to his office, Michael admitted to himself that he was angry. Not at Casey, but at himself. He should be able to tell her he loved her, to promise he'd always be there. But he didn't know if he could. It wasn't as if he didn't care about Casey, but he didn't know if what he felt was love.

Didn't she know that asking her to live with him was a huge step for him to take? He'd never even considered the possibility of a long-term relationship before. But he was more than willing to consider it now.

Still upset, Michael found Nathan pacing in his office when he got to work. One look at Nathan's face was more than enough to convince Michael something was wrong.

"The merger's going down the toilet," Nathan said without any preamble.

Michael set his briefcase on his desk, dread filling him. He knew he shouldn't have spent so much time away from the office. If he'd been spending his days at his desk, he could have prevented this.

"What happened?" he asked Nathan. "I vetted the company, and they seemed solid."

"They have lost interest. You realize what this means, don't you? If this merger falls through, we can't expand the way we've planned. That's a hundred jobs lost. The impact to the town will be huge."

Michael leaned against his desk, alternatives running through his mind. Unfortunately, he couldn't come up with any other solutions. Barrett Software needed this merger like a dying man needed a transfusion. They needed to get bigger, so they didn't end up being overwhelmed by the competition. "We have to save the deal."

Nathan stopped directly in front of him. "How? They've called off negotiations."

Michael was living his worst nightmare. He knew how to solve this problem, and it was killing him. Why did everything in life have to be so hard?

"They'll listen to me if I fly up there tonight and fix it," he said finally.

"Isn't your fundraiser thing tomorrow? I thought you had to be there," Nathan said.

Michael felt like alcohol had just been poured into a gaping wound in his heart. There was no way he could save the merger and be back in time for Big Band Night. Casey would never understand him missing the fundraiser. Moreover, he had wanted to be there, not only for her, but also for the seniors. Over the last few weeks, those people had come to mean a lot to him.

He looked at Nathan. He hated this, but he had no choice. Not really. Those employees needed him. If he didn't go up there and work this out, they would be out of work within a matter of weeks.

"It's more important I try to save the merger," Michael said. "I don't need to be at the dance."

"But Casey—"

"Will be fine," Michael said, knowing he was lying. She would never forgive him. He ran a weary hand through his hair. "I guess I can explain what's happening to her—"

"Not unless you want to get us in a real mess. You preannounce this merger, and we're in deep legal trouble," Nathan said.

"Casey won't tell anyone."

"Doesn't matter. You aren't allowed to tell anyone."

Michael nodded, knowing his boss was right. He couldn't tell her what was happening. Could this get any worse? Casey was going to hate him.

Nathan patted him on the arm, compassion evident on the older man's face. "Just tell her it's important business. I'm sure she'll understand."

Yeah, right. And pigs could learn to fly. "I doubt it," Michael said.

"Sure, she will. She cares about you. And I know

she means a lot to you, or you wouldn't be worried about what she'll think."

"Nathan, this morning, I asked Casey to live with me."

Surprise crossed Nathan's face. "Really? Good for you. Well, then, that's even more reason why she won't mind you missing the fundraiser. If she's willing to live with you, she knows how important your job is."

"She'll be devastated," Michael said, knowing it was true. Tomorrow night meant everything to Casey. How could he miss one of the most important nights of her life?

Nathan continued to watch him. "Maybe we could get someone else to—"

Michael waved away the suggestion. "No. It's my deal. I set it up. I vetted this company and made the recommendation, so I'll save it."

With a nod, Nathan headed toward the door. Right before he left, he turned and looked at Michael. "I'm proud of you, Michael. You've made the right choice."

"I know," Michael said. It was the right choice. But as he watched Nathan leave his office, he knew there was no way Casey would understand. She'd think he'd chosen business over her, and she wouldn't understand.

He knew it as well as he knew his own name.

Casey half expected the knock on her door about an hour after she got home. Michael hadn't said he was going to stop by, but she wasn't surprised he had. They needed to talk, but boy, was she dreading this conversation.

Peering through the peephole, she saw him standing outside, and the butterflies in her stomach turned into giant flying bats. Taking a deep breath, she tried to calm her nerves and opened the door. Why did love have to be so complicated? As much as she wanted to tell him that she would live with him, she just wasn't certain it would work.

One look at Michael's expression, and her anxiety was immediately replaced with fear. Cold, alone-in-the-house-with-a-psycho fear. Something bad had happened.

"What's wrong?" She stepped aside so Michael could enter her apartment, but he remained standing in the doorway.

"I have to leave town for a couple of days," he said bluntly.

Casey sucked in a startled breath, feeling like he'd thrown a sucker punch. "What? Will you be back in time for Big Band Night?"

He shook his head. "I can't tell you how upset I am about this," he said. "I want to be there tomorrow, but a problem has come up at work, and I'm the only one who can solve it."

Casey's throat closed up. After everything they'd done, after all the plans, he was standing her up so he could go on a business trip. She'd heard this song played time and again while growing up. *Got to go. Be back sometime. Love ya.*

Yeah, right.

"I see," was all she said, all she could think to say. She leaned back against the wall, needing the support. How could he do this? More important, how could she have been so foolish as to fall for a workaholic? Sooner or later, corporate sharks always reverted to type. He had a right to make work his priority, but that wasn't the life she wanted to live.

"Casey, I don't want to go. I have to go. I want to be here with you," he said, his voice strained. "You think I'm like your parents, but I've changed. Right now, I don't want to be anywhere other than with you. But I can't let the Barrett Software employees down."

Casey registered the sincerity in his voice. She knew Michael felt he was doing the right thing by taking this trip. He truly believed he was doing it for the employees.

Normally, Casey would have cut him some slack, but she'd grown up hearing that same line year after lonely year. She didn't want to spend countless nights alone while the company took precedence.

And she wouldn't do it. She might love Michael, but she couldn't spend her life with him. If he would miss the fundraiser, knowing what it meant to her, then he would miss other important moments in their life together.

So she'd stop things right here, right now, no matter how much it hurt. In her mind, this breakup was like yanking a bandage off a cut. If she did it fast, the pain wouldn't hurt as much. Well, at least not in the long run.

"I don't think we should see each other anymore," she said softly, ignoring his loud protest at her words. "You have different priorities than I do, so I think—"

"Dammit, Casey, don't do this. I can't tell you why I won't be at the fundraiser. This trip is confidential. But you need to believe that I don't want to go. It's important."

"Big Band Night is important, too. Now if you'll excuse me, I don't think we have anything else to say to each other." She wasn't trying to be a witch, but she was adamant that this type of life wasn't for her.

"Casey." He sighed. "Sometimes it is difficult to fulfill all promises. You know that. You missed Elmira's birthday."

She wiped a couple of stray tears off her cheeks. Where had those come from? She never cried. Ever. And she wasn't going to start now, even if the anguish in his voice made her heart constrict. "I know. I did. And I regret it."

"Don't do this," Michael said again. "I know now I love you."

Casey smiled wryly. "I love you, too. Except love isn't enough. I'm not trying to hurt you, but I really think we need to stop things now, before we fall even more in love."

Not daring to risk the possibility that Michael might say something to weaken her resolve, she moved to shut the door. "I have to go."

He slapped his palm against the door, keeping it open. "I can't send someone else. This is my responsibility."

Her tone was soft as she said, "I know. I understand. And being responsible is one of the great things about you. But I know what kind of life I want to live, Michael. It's a simple life that doesn't involve emergency meetings and endless promotions. I want to enjoy my life, and I want a man who will enjoy it with me. You need to go do what you have to do."

They stood, for timeless moments, facing each other across the threshold. Casey knew how much it had cost Michael to admit that he loved her, and his admission made her heart break even more. He was a good man who wouldn't mean to hurt her. But he would always choose business.

Silently, she pushed on the door. This time, Michael didn't stop her. He let go, and the door swung shut. And once it was closed, Casey realized it was over. It had only been a matter of time before this happened. She should have known better than to fall for a man like Michael. Whenever you needed them most, they were always somewhere else.

More tears threatened to fall, but she held them back. She would not cry. Not about this. But the dampness on her cheeks was making a liar out of her. Finally, a couple of tears broke free and ran down her cheeks. Drat. She was tough. She was strong. She didn't want to cry over a man. But when more tears escaped, she decided to give up the fight.

This was going to hurt.

Dragging in a deep breath, she headed to the living room, snagging a handful of tissues before she curled up on the sofa. She'd done the right thing. Someday, she'd find someone else. She'd fall in love again.

Maybe he wouldn't be quite as handsome as Michael. And maybe his hair wouldn't droop across his forehead in that cute way Michael's did. And maybe he wouldn't make her laugh like Michael could. But he'd still be a great guy. And he'd be there for her. And for their children.

He just wouldn't be Michael.

That thought twisted her heart, but she reined in her grief. She could be strong about this. She would be strong about this.

After all, no one had ever died of a broken heart.

◌⟡◌

"Would you like something to drink?"

Michael looked up at the flight attendant and shook his head. "No, thanks." After she wheeled her cart away, he turned his attention back to the window next to him. Normally, he loved to fly. He enjoyed the thought of being so far above the ground. But today, he couldn't relax. All he could think about was Casey and what had happened between them.

He'd finally told a woman he loved her, and she'd literally shut the door in his face. Not that he could blame her. She'd made it clear to him several times how important it was that he be there for her. And he'd wanted, more than anything, to be there tomorrow.

But the merger was just too important. Wasn't this just like life? Here he'd finally found a woman to love, and he'd had to toss her love away for work. This was what he'd tried to avoid all along with Casey —this feeling of guilt, of remorse. He'd never resented his job until today. He loved working for Barrett Software, seeing the profits grow and the company expand. But right now, he'd give anything to be back home. With her.

Except countless new jobs depended on him, not to mention the jobs of the current employees. He couldn't throw them away. Those jobs represented the hopes and dreams of other people. And those people trusted him. So he had to do what he could to save their jobs.

As much as he liked to think he could convince Casey to reconsider when he got back home, he knew he had a better chance of sprouting wings and flying to Michigan himself. Her parents had laid the groundwork for her prejudice against corporate execs, and he'd finished the job. Part of what he loved about Casey was her determination. But now that determination would cost him everything. She wouldn't change her mind, wouldn't give him an inch. Nope, Casey Richards was one tough lady.

But what had he expected? He'd known all along he wasn't cut out for love. He couldn't finally discover love at thirty-two and be any good at it. Besides, Casey was right. This trip wouldn't be the last emergency he'd face during his career. There would be plenty more. Another crisis or emergency or opportunity. He'd have to be there. He'd have to be free to hop on a plane and go where he was needed without worrying about hurting someone. He couldn't spend his life constantly making those kinds of choices.

He also knew it wasn't fair to expect someone to always let him leave. No woman deserved to be left alone all the time. That wasn't love, and it wasn't a life. Casey deserved so much more than he could offer her.

No, she was right. They'd both be better off if things ended here. Sure, he'd hurt for a while. She'd hurt, too, and that thought made him almost frantic. But in the end, in a while, they'd both be better off. He'd have the promotion and everything he'd ever worked for, and Casey would have the new center and probably find another man who would be there for her.

That thought made Michael's stomach drop. Another man with Casey. Holding her. Loving her. Having children with her.

Man, he hated his job right now. Almost as much as he hated himself.

❀

"Wow, this place looks like a fairyland," Dottie said, tugging Casey farther into the cafeteria. "Barrett Software sure knows how to throw a party."

Casey glanced around and had to agree. With silver and white decorations everywhere and small twinkling lights cascading down the walls, the room did resemble something out of a story. Every table was draped in a cream linen tablecloth and had an impressive pink, purple, and white flower centerpiece with a large flickering candle in the center.

The decorations were so much more than she had hoped for. When she'd showed up this morning, she'd found a professional crew already at work.

The foreman of the group explained that Barrett Software often held large functions in this room and had the necessary supplies. When she saw Nathan tonight, she would thank him for his generosity.

"It does look pretty terrific," Casey agreed. "Plus, it's a good thing we've got a room this big. Michael and Nathan have invited everyone they know."

"Hey, what about me?" Dottie put her hands on her hips. "I rustled up more than a few people for you by using some heavy guilt on all my relatives. After this, I'll be getting fruitcake from everyone at Christmas."

Casey chuckled. "I appreciate your sacrifice."

"No problem." Dottie squeezed her arm. "I'm really sorry about Michael. Are you okay?"

Casey nodded. "Sure. I'm going to have a great time. Why don't you go mingle?"

Dottie studied her face. "Are you sure? Because I can stay with you if—"

Shaking her head, Casey nudged her friend toward the crowd. "No. Go. I'm fine."

After Dottie walked away, Casey rubbed a nervous hand against the side of her calf-length black dress. Getting ready for the party had been a nightmare. She'd run two pairs of tights, smeared her eyeliner, and been unable to get her hair into a bun. Finally, she'd decided to forgo the tights, taken off the eyeliner, and decided to leave her hair loose. She was in no mood to fight with anything tonight.

Glancing around the room, she realized couples were starting to drift in, so she went over to greet them. Everyone looked so terrific, all dressed up for the party. The seniors, especially, had dressed to the hilt. She spotted both Tommy and Al wearing tuxedos, while several of the women had on glittering long dresses.

Casey was too jumpy to sit while dinner was served. She circled the room, making certain everything was perfect. Finally, after the plates were removed, the band arrived and launched into a loud, upbeat song.

Smiles covered each face, and Casey knew she had

to smile back, so she did, but she found it difficult pretending to be happy. As much as she hated to admit it, she was downright miserable. She missed Michael and desperately wanted him next to her tonight.

For the millionth time, she berated herself for being silly enough to fall in love with a workaholic. She, of all people, should have known better. Of course, he'd chosen his job over her. Even if he'd wanted to choose her, his job required him to choose it. High-powered jobs always did.

"Looks like the party should bring in some serious cash," Nathan said next to her.

Casey turned and shook his hand. She met his wife, Emma. Then she smiled at Benjamin and Elmira, who also stood by Nathan's side. Elmira's hand was resting on Benjamin's arm. Apparently, their romance was progressing far better than her own had with Michael.

"I'm keeping my fingers crossed. You and Michael sure convinced a lot of people to come. The advance ticket sales alone had almost brought in enough money. And thankfully, we're getting quite a few last-minute attendees, so we should be all right." She smiled at Elmira. "You're looking beautiful tonight."

Beautiful was an understatement. The older woman practically beamed with happiness. Dressed in a floor-length blue velvet gown, Elmira looked elegant.

"Thank you, Casey. I'm having a wonderful time." Elmira looked around. "Where's Michael?"

Apparently, she hadn't heard the news yet. Before Casey could answer, Nathan said, "He had to go away on business."

Mouth open, Elmira looked up at Nathan. "You sent him away the night of the party?"

To give him credit, Nathan seemed unruffled by her question. "I didn't send him. He made his own choice. But it was vital he go."

His wife, father-in-law, and Elmira were all frowning at Nathan, so Casey decided to cut him some slack.

"It was important that Michael went," she echoed. "He is very responsible."

Casey resisted the impulse to follow Nathan and ask him to explain just what was so vital it couldn't wait twenty-four hours. Surely Michael could have caught a plane after the party if he'd wanted to. It was the weekend. Who worked on the weekend? Well, other than a workaholic.

Glancing over at the dance floor, she watched the couples dance. Benjamin and Elmira seemed so happy. The couple danced together as if they'd been doing it for years. Standing alone, Casey couldn't help feeling happy for them and sad for herself.

She looked over. Nathan and his wife were also dancing and looking very happy. Nathan had managed to be here tonight. He hadn't been called away on some last-minute business.

She would have loved to have Michael hold her like that and spin her around the dance floor. She felt her eyes misting and struggled to remain in control. But she wouldn't cry anymore. Her pity party was officially over.

Deciding to dry her eyes before any tears fell, she hurried toward the bathroom, hoping no one saw her. She wouldn't ruin tonight, no matter what had happened with Michael.

Tonight was too important to spoil.

H e was going to be late, Michael decided with a curse. He increased his speed, running through the airport for all he was worth. Until now, he'd thought he was in pretty good shape, but sprinting for a plane was the way to find out if he was.

Reaching the gate just as they were shutting the door, he hollered for them to wait and handed his boarding pass to the startled gate agent.

"You're cutting it close, aren't you?" she asked.

"You have no idea," Michael said. He grabbed the stub from her and hurried down the jetway toward the plane.

"Glad we didn't leave without you," the flight attendant said when he stepped inside the plane. "Let's get you in your seat."

Glancing at Michael's boarding pass, the attendant directed him to the remaining empty seat in first class. Michael shoved his small suitcase in the overhead compartment and dropped into his seat. He'd actually made it. He hadn't thought he had a chance when he'd grabbed a cab to the airport a half an hour ago.

But luck had been with him. There'd been a seat left in first class, so Michael had taken it, regardless of the cost.

Unable to stop himself, he smiled. If the winds were with him, he should make it back in time to catch some of the party. Maybe he even could convince Casey to share a dance with him.

That was, if she didn't mind dancing with a man who'd just thrown away his chance of a promotion. Oh, he'd done his job, all right.

He'd started the meeting at six this morning and kept things moving until they'd pounded out an agreement a little over an hour ago. Once he knew the deal would go through and the jobs were secure, he'd turned it over to Glenda. Now Glenda would put the final shine on the package and get all the glory.

She deserved that chance to show off her skills. She deserved a promotion.

But Michael no longer cared if he got promoted. He'd sat in the meeting and realized he didn't want to be a hotshot executive if he couldn't have Casey. He'd find another job before he gave her up.

The sentiment had seized him with such urgency that he knew better than to ignore it. For years, he'd worked his butt off. He was successful, but he had nothing to show for all those years except a big bank account and an empty life.

Until he'd met Casey. Now he knew he had a new focus in life. A life that he hoped would include Casey, and someday, children. She'd told him the night they'd first made love that she was proud of him.

Today, when he'd decided to come home to Casey and left the meeting early, he'd been proud of himself, too. All he had to do was convince Casey to give him another chance. But this time, he wasn't going halfway. He wasn't just going to ask her to live with him.

He was going to ask her to marry him.

"Nathan would like to dance with you," Elmira said, coming into the ladies' room.

Casey dabbed at her cheeks with a tissue, wiping away the rest of her tears. Checking her reflection, she realized her eyes were still slightly red, but there was nothing she could do about it. With luck, it was dark enough at the party that no one would see. Elmira noticed, though, and she frowned at Casey's reflection in the mirror.

"Don't cry. Things will work out."

"I'm not—"

"Yes, you are," Elmira said, moving forward and taking Casey's hand. "You're crying about Michael, aren't you? Casey, men are like flypaper. Once you're stuck on them, it's hard to break free."

Casey smiled ruefully. "Guess I'm a fool, aren't I?"

With a shake of her head, Elmira nudged Casey toward the door. "No. Just a woman in love. Now get out of here and go dance with Nathan. He told me he wants to talk to you."

Casey followed the older woman from the bathroom. They walked over to where Nathan stood with his wife at the edge of the dance floor.

"Come on, let's dance," Nathan said to Casey.

Uncertain, Casey looked at his wife, Emma. "I don't want to interrupt."

Emma waved them off. "Don't worry about me. I'd like to sit for a while and visit with the ladies."

Glancing at Elmira, Casey said, "Be certain and get me before they auction the car."

Elmira nodded, her hand resting on Benjamin's arm. "I won't forget."

A look passed between Elmira and Benjamin that made Casey wonder if these two might end up together. They had already developed a shorthand that only those in love seemed to have.

When Nathan took her hand, Casey followed him out to the crowded dance floor. A lot more people had arrived in the past few minutes.

"The party is going to make more than enough money for the modifications," Nathan said, smiling. "Businessman that I am, I went and checked on the total while you ladies were talking. Your fundraiser is a hit."

"That's wonderful." Casey smiled, genuinely pleased. Now the new center could have all the facilities she'd always dreamed of. Of course, it would take a lot of work to make the changes to the house, but she didn't mind. They'd find a good contractor and some talented workers, and she would work with them to make certain everything was perfect.

"And you haven't even auctioned off the car yet," Nathan pointed out. "That should bring in even more money."

"I hope so," Casey said. Michael had already had the car appraised, and all the seniors had agreed to pay Elmira top dollar for her late husband's pride and joy.

"So, your party's a huge success, but you look really sad, as if your best friend ran away with your dog. What's the problem?" Nathan asked.

"I'm not sad," she protested.

Nathan snorted. "Try that one again. My wife noticed it right away, but even a fairly clueless guy like me can see it a mile off. You can smile to beat the band, but those smiles aren't real. I should know—as a boss, I get lots of fake smiles flashed at me all day long. So what's wrong? Emma thinks you're upset about Michael. Is that true?"

Casey's gaze met his. She could lie, but there didn't seem much point. "Yes. After all he's done for this fundraiser, I'd hoped he'd be here."

Through narrowed eyes, Nathan appraised her. "Didn't Michael explain he had to go? You know he wanted to be here."

"I can't help thinking if he'd really wanted to be here, he would be," she said, hoping Nathan would drop it. Despite everything that had happened, she didn't want to criticize Michael in front of his boss.

"No offense, but a fat lot you know about business," Nathan said, leading her through a series of intricate steps. When they settled back into a normal rhythm, she frowned at him.

"I may not know about business, but I know people. Michael made a choice. He wanted to impress you, to get another promotion," she said quietly, the truth of her words causing a new wave of pain to go through her. "That promotion's worth more to him than I am."

Nathan stopped dancing. He ignored all the other couples swirling around them and just stood, staring at Casey. "Excuse me, Casey. I like you, so take this the way it's intended, but you don't know diddly-squat."

Casey blinked. She should have known another corporate CEO wouldn't understand. "I think I do. Michael decided to go on the business trip rather than to be here."

"So he didn't tell you why he had to go?"

She shrugged, feeling self-conscious. "He said it was important, but this is important too."

"The trip wasn't just important to Michael.

Around a hundred new jobs will be created, and the folks who already work at Barrett Software will have much greater job security."

Stunned, Casey looked up at Nathan. "What?"

"Casey, Michael went because it was the right thing to do. The guy was in a tough spot, between a rock and..." He grinned. "And you. But in the end, he went because he had to. Sure, you would have liked him here with you, but those employees needed him at these meetings."

"Really?"

He cocked one eyebrow. "Why? Did you give him a hard time about going?"

A hard time? That was an understatement. "I broke things off with him."

"Man, that's rough." Nathan took her hand and started dancing again. "I thought you were in love with Michael."

"I am." She swallowed and amended her answer. "I mean, I was."

"Was? Past tense?"

At his dubious expression, she relented. "Okay, I am. I'm still in love with him."

"Then you should feel proud of him. He made a tough decision, but the right one. Those employees have families. A lot of people depend on him." He smiled at her. "Michael's changed in the last few weeks, Casey."

She saw that now. Michael wasn't a thing like her parents. Her parents had worked so hard because

LORI WILDE & LIZ ALVIN

they wanted to get promotions—for themselves. Michael had left her because he'd needed to do this. Or had he?

"But if he pulls this off, won't he end up getting promoted?" she asked.

Nathan chuckled. "You're one tough lady. Maybe. It's up to me. But there's more to being an executive at Barrett Software than just putting in the hours. You have to have heart; you have to care about people."

Casey nibbled her bottom lip, suddenly uncertain. Had Michael really gone on the trip to save those jobs or because he thought he'd get a promotion? She wouldn't know if she didn't ask Michael.

"I should call him," she said, needing to know.

"No. Michael's in nonstop meetings this weekend. You should wait until he gets back and talk to him in person." With that, Nathan finished the dance and then led her over to the table where Emma, Benjamin, and Elmira sat.

Nathan asked, "You folks ready to do this auction?"

Casey went to the band, borrowed the microphone, and gathered the group. Then Tommy, who used to be an auctioneer, climbed on stage, cracked a few jokes about the supposedly magical car, and began the auction. Bidding started out slow, and for a while, Casey worried that they wouldn't earn back the money the center had promised Elmira.

Then, as if a dam had burst, the bidding took

off. Three men were in heavy competition, each upping the amount by several hundred with each bid.

Finally, the competition dropped to only two bidders, and eventually, it became clear one man would win. The man's final bid wasn't as much as Casey had hoped for, but it would do nicely.

Tommy raised his gavel to accept the final bid when, from the back of the room, a man said, "Fifty thousand dollars."

A gasp went through the room. Casey recognized that voice. Or at least, she thought she did. She searched the crowd, looking for the benefactor. Finally, the crowd parted enough so she could see Michael walking toward the stage.

She borrowed the microphone from Tommy.

"Are you certain?" she asked Michael, love filling her. He'd come back. To her.

"I'm positive," he said loudly enough for Casey to hear.

Tommy laughed and slammed the gavel on the podium. "That's good enough for me. I'm calling this before that man changes his mind."

Bemused, Casey stepped down from the platform and crossed the room. When she stood directly in front of Michael, she said, "I didn't know you liked antique cars."

"I didn't," he smiled down at her, a teasing twinkle in his sexy blue eyes. "Until recently. But I've become a believer in the magic of that car."

Dancing started again, so the crowd wandered off as Casey continued to stare at Michael.

"Looks like the evening was a huge success," Michael said.

Casey nodded, still unable to believe he'd come back. Still a little uncertain why he had. "Yes. We made more than enough money."

Michael took a step toward her, his gaze holding hers. "Casey, I want—"

She couldn't stand it anymore. She rose up on her toes and pressed her lips to his. When he didn't kiss her back at first, she decided he was surprised, so she brushed his lips again. This time, Michael pulled her close, his head bending to her, his lips seeking hers in a deep kiss.

He'd come back. He'd left his meeting and come back to her. Abruptly, she realized what that meant and leaned back from the temptation of his kiss.

"The meeting. The jobs," she whispered, floundering.

"I hurried things along, but I got it settled enough to leave." He cupped her face, his eyes glittering as they studied her face. "I had to go, Casey. I didn't want to—"

She laid a finger across his mouth. "I know. I realize that now. You made the right choice."

Before she moved her finger away, he nipped playfully at it, making Casey laugh. Then he took her hand in his, tugging her close again.

"I love you, Casey Richards. I'll do anything for you."

Lovingly, she gazed into his eyes. "I love you, too."

He kissed her again, tenderly, then said, "But you have to know before we go any further that I've decided I don't want to live together."

Her stomach dropped. "If you're not ready—"

Shaking his head, he said, "I want to get married. I want to spend the rest of my life with you. Say you'll marry me. I promise I won't let my career come before what's really important in life—you."

"Now how can I resist a promise like that? Yes, I'll marry you," she murmured against his lips. He rewarded her with a thorough and enthusiastic kiss.

"One more thing," he said when he ended the kiss. "I hope you didn't have your heart set on me getting promoted. By leaving the meeting early, I'll probably get chewed out big-time. In fact, I'll be lucky if I'm not demoted because of this."

"I don't care," Casey assured him. "But I know how much it means to you." She caressed the side of his face. He didn't look unhappy. He looked ecstatic.

"Not me. Not anymore. Sure, I want to do a good job, but it's more important to have a life—a life that you're a part of. No more workaholic days for me."

A new thought occurred to her. "Michael, with the new center, I may have to put in some long days."

He grinned. "Okay, I'll work late when you work late. Then we can meet back home and see if we can get into trouble."

"We can only get into trouble on the nights we work late?" she teased.

Michael leaned forward and started to murmur something naughty in her ear, but before he could, Nathan said, "Hi, Michael. Hi, Casey."

They moved slightly apart and turned to face him.

"I guess you've heard from Glenda that I decided to leave after we worked through the major details," Michael told his boss. "And I stand by my decision, Nathan, even though I know it will reflect on my career."

Michael glanced at Casey. "It was important for me to be here tonight. Glenda will do a great job finalizing the deal. I asked her if she wanted to stay, and she said yes. She'd like to be considered for a promotion."

Nathan laughed. "I think that's great, and I agree, Glenda deserves a promotion. And it doesn't bother me that you left. I'm all for delegating. I'm a firm believer in sharing the workload so no one ends up having to do everything." He wrapped his arm around his wife's waist, then turned his attention back to Michael. Casey could see the love radiating off the other couple.

"Truthfully," Nathan said, "I think you did a great job. You've always had the brains and the talent, but frankly, I worried that you lacked heart." He smiled. "I see now, you've got that, too. The promotion is yours."

Next to her, Casey felt Michael stiffen. "Nathan, I can't put in crazy hours."

"So don't. Spread the work around. Hire an assistant or two. You'll need to anyway because Glenda will also be getting promoted. You don't have to do all the work personally. Live your life at the same time. You only get one."

With that, Nathan patted Michael's arm and headed back to the dance floor with his wife. Stunned, Casey looked up at Michael and laughed when she saw the bemused expression on his handsome face.

"I have to agree with him. You certainly have a heart," she said.

He pulled her close, hugging her. "I do now. Thanks to you."

"You are the most perfect man," she said quietly, cupping his face.

He chuckled and shook his head. "Me? Perfect?"

"Yep," she whispered, standing on tiptoe to press her lips to his. "You're perfect for me, hotshot."

❧

Dear Reader,

Readers are an author's life blood and the stories couldn't happen without you. Thank you so much for reading! If you enjoyed *Handsome Hotshot,* we would so appreciate a review. You have no idea how much it means to us.

If you'd like to keep up with our latest releases, you can sign up for Lori's newsletter @ https://loriwilde.com/sign-up/.

Please turn the page for an excerpt for the first book in the The Handsome Devil series *Handsome Rancher.*

To check out our other books, you can visit us on the web @ www.loriwilde.com.

Love and light,

Lori and Liz

EXCERPT: HANDSOME RANCHER

As she studied him, standing near the entrance to the city council room, Megan Kendall couldn't help thinking what a handsome devil Chase Barrett was.

Everyone in the small town of Honey, Texas, thought so as well. With his drop-dead gorgeous looks and his handsome-devil smile, women fell for him like pine trees knocked down by a powerful tornado.

Even Megan couldn't claim to be immune. She and Chase had been good friends for over twenty years, and he still didn't know she was madly in love with him.

Yep, he was a handsome devil all right.

"Picture him naked," Leigh Barrett whispered to Megan.

Stunned, Megan turned to stare at Chase's younger sister. "Excuse me?"

Thankfully, Leigh nodded toward the front of the room instead of in her brother's direction. "The mayor. When you're giving your presentation, if you get nervous, picture him naked."

Megan slipped her glasses down her nose and studied Earl Guthrie, the seventy-three-year-old mayor of Honey. When Earl caught her gaze, he gave Megan a benign, vague smile.

"I don't think so," Megan said to Leigh. "I prefer to think of Earl as fully clothed."

Leigh giggled. "Okay, maybe that wasn't such a hot idea after all. Let me see if I can find someone else for you to think of naked."

"That's not necessary. I'm not nervous." Megan flipped through her index cards.

Her argument was flawless, her plan foolproof. She had nothing to be nervous about. Besides, as the head librarian of the Honey Library, she knew every person in the room. This presentation would be a snap.

But with puppy-like enthusiasm, Leigh had already stood and was looking around. She hadn't spotted her oldest brother yet, but Megan knew it was only a matter of time before she did.

"Leigh, I'm fine," Megan tried, but Leigh finally saw Chase and yelled at him to come over and join them.

Chase made his way through the crowded room. The city council meetings usually drew a big audience, but Megan was happy to see even more people than usual had turned out to listen to her presentation of fundraiser ideas for new playground equipment.

When Chase got even with Megan and Leigh, he leaned across Megan to ruffle his sister's dark hair. Then he dropped into the folding chair next to Megan and winked at her. "Ladies, how are you tonight?"

Megan tried to keep her expression pleasant, but it wasn't easy. Ever since she'd moved back to Honey last year, pretending her feelings for Chase were platonic was proving harder and harder. At six-two, with deep black hair and even deeper blue eyes, he made her heart race and her palms sweat.

"Don't ruffle my hair, bozo." Leigh huffed at Megan's right, smoothing her hair. "I'm in college. I'm too old to have my hair ruffled."

To Megan's left, Chase chuckled. "Squirt, you're never going to be too old for me to ruffle your hair. When you're eighty, I'm going to totter up to you and do it."

"You and what orderly?" Leigh teased. "And just for the record, I like Nathan and Trent much better than I like you."

"Oh, please." Megan rolled her eyes at that one. Leigh loved all of her brothers, but everyone knew Chase was her favorite. When she was home from college, she always stayed with Chase.

"I love you, too, squirt," Chase said, not rising to his sister's taunt. Instead, he nudged Megan. "You okay?"

"I told her to imagine the mayor naked if she got nervous, but she doesn't want to do that," Leigh supplied.

"I can see why not," Chase said. "Earl's not exactly stud-muffin material."

"Oooh, I know what she should do." Leigh practically bounced in her chair. "Megan, if you get nervous, picture Chase naked."

Megan froze and willed herself to stay calm. The absolute last thing she wanted to think about was Chase naked. Okay, maybe she did want to think of him naked, but not right now. Not right before she had to speak in front of a large portion of the entire town.

"I don't think so," Megan muttered, shooting a glare at Leigh.

The younger woman knew how Megan felt about her brother, and this was simply one more not-so-subtle attempt to get the two of them together. In the past few months, Leigh's matchmaking maneuvers had grown more extreme.

"I don't think I'll need to picture anyone naked," Megan stated.

On her other side, Chase offered, "Well, if you get

flustered and it will make things easier for you, you go ahead and think of me naked, Megan. Whatever I can do to help."

Megan knew Chase was teasing her, but suddenly she realized how many years she'd wasted waiting for him to take her seriously.

She'd fallen for him when she'd moved to town at eight. Dreamed about him since she'd turned sixteen. And tried like the dickens to forget him when she'd been away at college and then later working at a library in Dallas for five years.

But nothing had helped. Not even seriously dating a man in Dallas had helped. In her soul, Megan believed she and Chase were meant to be together.

If only she could get him to notice her.

"Hey there, Chase," a smooth, feline voice fairly purred over their shoulders. "You're looking yummy. Like an especially luscious dessert, and I positively love dessert."

Oh, great. Megan glanced behind her. Janet Defries. Just what she needed tonight.

Chase smiled at the woman half leaning on his chair. "Hey, Janet. Do you plan on helping Megan with her committee?"

From the look on Janet's face, the only thing she planned on helping herself to was Chase, served on a platter.

She leaned toward Chase, the position no doubt deliberate since a generous amount of cleavage was exposed. "Are you going to help with this committee, Chase? Because if you are, I might be able to pry free a few hours."

Yeah, right. Megan shared a glance with Leigh. They both knew Janet would no more help with the committee than dogs would sing.

"I'd like to help, but it's a busy time on the ranch," Chase said.

"Shame." Janet slipped into the chair directly behind him. "I think you and I should figure out a way to spend some quality time together."

Her message couldn't have been clearer if she'd plastered it on a billboard. Megan hated herself for wanting to know, but she couldn't not look. She turned to see what Chase's reaction was to the woman's blatant come-on.

Mild interest. Megan repressed a sigh. Of course. Janet was exactly the type of woman Chase favored. One with a high-octane body and zero interest in a lasting relationship.

"Maybe we'll figure it out one of these days," Chase said, and Megan felt her temperature climb.

Okay, so she didn't have a drawer at home full of D-cups, but Megan knew she could make Chase happy. She could make him believe in love again.

If the dimwit would give her the chance.

Janet placed one hand on Chase's arm and licked her lips. "Well, you hurry up, else I might decide to go after Nathan or Trent instead. You're not the only handsome fella in your family."

Chase chuckled as he faced forward in his chair once again. "I sure am being threatened with my brothers tonight. But I'd like to point out that neither of them stopped by to lend their support, and I'm sitting here like an angel."

Leigh snorted. "Angel? You? Give me a break. You could make the devil himself blush, Chase Barrett."

Chase's grin was pure male satisfaction. "I do my best."

As Megan knew only too well. She'd watched him beguile a large percentage of the females in this part of Texas. Why couldn't he throw a little of that wickedness her way? Just once, she'd like to show him how combustible they could be together.

But even though she'd been back in Honey for almost a year, the man still treated her like a teenager. She'd just celebrated her twenty-ninth birthday. She wasn't a sheltered virgin with fairy-tale dreams of romance. She was a flesh and blood woman who knew what she wanted out of life.

She wanted Chase.

After a great deal of commotion getting the microphone to the right level, the mayor finally started the meeting. Within a few minutes, it was time for her presentation. Megan stood, adjusting her glasses.

"Remember, picture Chase naked if you get nervous," Leigh whispered but not very softly.

Megan was in the process of scooting past Chase, who had stood to let her by. She froze, standing directly in front of the man who consumed her dreams and starred in her fantasies.

He grinned.

"You know, I think I just may do that," Megan said. "And if he gets nervous, he can picture me naked, too."

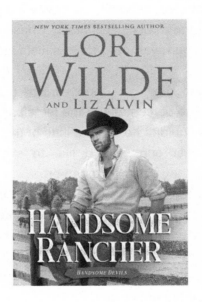

ABOUT THE AUTHORS

Liz Alvin

Liz Alvin has loved reading and writing for as long as she can remember. In fact, she majored in literature at college just so she could spend her days reading great stories. When it came to her own stories, she decided to write romances with happy endings because she's a firm believer in love. She's been married to her own hero for over 30 years. They live in Texas near their adult children and are surrounded by rescue dogs and a rescue cat.

Lori Wilde

Lori Wilde is the New York Times, USA Today and Publishers' Weekly bestselling author of 88 works of romantic fiction. She's a three time Romance Writers' of America RITA finalist and has four times been nominated for Romantic Times Readers' Choice Award. She has won numerous other awards as well.

Her books have been translated into 26 languages, with more than four million copies of her books sold worldwide.

Her breakout novel, *The First Love Cookie Club*, has been optioned for a TV movie.

Lori is a registered nurse with a BSN from Texas Christian University. She holds a certificate in forensics, and is also a certified yoga instructor.

A fifth generation Texan, Lori lives with her husband, Bill, in the Cutting Horse Capital of the World; where they run Epiphany Orchards, a writing/creativity retreat for the care and enrichment of the artistic soul.

Made in the USA
Las Vegas, NV
09 March 2021